GUARDIANS
of GA'HOOLE
THE LEGENDS

The First Collier

GUARDIANS
of GA'HOOLE
THE LEGENDS

BOOK NINE

The First Collier

BY KATHRYN LASKY

SCHOLASTIC INC.

New York Toronto London Auckland Sydney
Mexico City New Delhi Hong Kong Buenos Aires

ISBN 0-439-79568-0

Text copyright © 2006 by Kathryn Lasky. Art copyright © 2006 by Scholastic Inc. All rights reserved. Published by Scholastic Inc. SCHOLASTIC and associated logos are trademarks and/or registered trademarks of Scholastic Inc.

Design by Steve Scott

12 11 10 9 8 7 6 5 4 3 2 1   6 7 8 9 10 11/0

Printed in the U.S.A.   40

First printing, April 2006

To Craig Walker,
the *Guardian*
K. L.

Contents

Prologue

On a branch outside a hollow of the Great Ga'Hoole Tree, three owls hunched against the first blasts of an early winter gale. One was an Elf Owl, one a Great Gray, and one a Burrowing Owl. They were known collectively as the Band, but their fourth member, the Barn Owl Soren, was in the hollow of his beloved old teacher, Ezylryb. And Ezylryb was dying.

The little Elf Owl Gylfie huddled close to Twilight and the huge Great Gray extended his wing to shelter her from the wind. Digger crept closer to them on the branch. Although Soren was inside and they were out, it was as if they were connected. These four owls who had known one another for so long could never really be separated.

"I feel it all," Gylfie said, and she blinked. "It's almost as if our gizzards are one."

Twilight and Digger nodded. "All of our gizzards," Digger whispered. And they, indeed, were feeling in that most sensitive of all owl organs the terrible grief that was racking their dear friend's gizzard as he stood by his old mentor. "I know it sounds silly," Digger said. "But it's almost like being orphaned again. And for Soren, it really must feel that way. I mean, after all, he is Ezylryb's ward."

Twilight blinked. "I don't remember being orphaned. I can't even remember my parents. I think I hatched by myself."

If he says something about the orphan school of tough learning and how he taught himself everything, I'll yarp, *Gylfie thought.*

But Twilight didn't. "And even though I can't remember any of that," he continued, "I think I can almost feel what it would have been like to have a father, to be a son. Poor Soren!"

Inside the hollow, Soren might have dimly sensed the tremors in his dear friends' gizzards, but, in truth, he let himself be swept to some unreachable place in a tidal wave of grief. His glistening black eyes turned dull. A peculiar stillness took hold of his gizzard. He was numb, almost yeep.

Octavia, Ezylryb's nest-maid snake, was coiled up in a corner weeping as her old master lay dying. Coryn, the new king of the great tree and leader of the Guardians, shifted nervously from one foot to the other. The young Barn Owl felt odd being in the old ryb's hollow. He felt out of place. He was new to the tree and had no history with Ezylryb, as did Octavia and his uncle, Soren.

Octavia had arrived with the Whiskered Screech countless years before and had served as his nest-maid and closest confidante as long as any owl could remember. Soren had been adopted by Ezylryb as his ward when he was quite young. Ezylryb had sensed the remarkable genius for leadership in the young Barn Owl even before Soren was aware of his own natural abilities. Coryn, though he was king, felt he did not belong here at this moment. But Ezylryb had summoned him along with Soren. Now the old ryb raised one mangled foot, and with it he beckoned the two Barn Owls to his side.

"Step closer, lads. Step closer," he whispered hoarsely.

It made Coryn feel good that Ezylryb had called him "lad." The old owl had used no title except "lad" to address the young king since he had arrived a short time before.

Now Coryn and Soren bent close to the old ryb's beak. "Listen closely to what I have to say."

"Yes, Ezylryb, I am listening," Coryn replied.

"Yes, Cap," Soren whispered. This was the last time he would call the old ryb "Cap." Everyone in the weather interpretation chaw called Ezylryb "Cap," for he had been the ultimate captain of the winds, teaching them how to ride the baggywrinkles and navigate the troughs and scuppers of a gale. Oh, what wild flights they'd had — through every kind of weather, every sort of boisterous wind. And always singing those riotous songs! Is that what he would miss most? Soren thought. Or perhaps he would most miss the talks that went long into the day; or the times in the library when Ezylryb would direct him to a book with that mangled talon. Great Glaux, he had learned so much from the old Whiskered Screech. So much!

Ezylryb tried to raise himself up from the downy pillow.

"Ezylryb," Soren said gently, "rest."

"No, Soren. I can't rest until I tell you both this. I know we have defeated the owls of St. Aggie's, destroyed their great stores of flecks. And, thank Glaux, the Pure Ones have been decimated. But who knows what evil might be lying in wait?" Ezylryb's breath became more labored. "The ember has returned to the Great Tree." His voice was now barely a whisper. Soren and his nephew tipped their heads closer to the old ryb's beak. "It brings great promise . . . and great danger. Ignorance is perhaps the source of all evil. Forget battle claws, forget ice swords and ice daggers. Knowledge is the most powerful weapon of all. It is vitally important that you know how we came to be, the stories even older than the cantos, the legends of Ga'Hoole. You must learn from that brilliant prince, that knight in the times of magic, who became our king Hoole, and whose ember, you, Coryn, and you alone, retrieved from the volcanoes of Beyond the Beyond. You must both read the oldest of the legends."

"We'll go to the library at once, sir," Coryn replied.

"No, no." He shook that mangled foot with more vigor than he had shown in a long time. "They are not in the library. They are here in a secret place in this hollow." He nodded at Soren. "He knows."

Yes, Soren did know. Within this hollow, there was a secret chamber that Soren and Gylife had discovered years before. It was where they had found Ezylryb's old battle claws, the ones that Ezylryb gave to Soren when he made Soren his ward. And there were books in that chamber and ancient scrolls from Ezylryb's homeland, the ancient Northern Kingdoms.

"Read them. Read them and learn," Ezylryb said. "Read them and know where we came from . . . and what we must guard against. The future is yours if . . ."

But he never finished what he had begun to say. His amber eyes slid back in his head. His beak was still. There was one last shallow breath. Then a light breeze blew through the hollow and with it a spirit passed. The old ryb was dead.

It was not until three days later after the Final ceremonies that Octavia led Coryn and Soren into the small hidden chamber behind Ezylryb's main hollow. Soren fetched the first of three ancient tomes. The two owls bent over the dusty old book. They had to squint to make out the faded gold letters of the title inscribed on the mouse-leather cover. THE LEGENDS OF GA'HOOLE, and then beneath this in smaller letters: THE FIRST COLLIER.

Soren opened the book and looked at his young nephew. They would read it together, slowly, carefully. And although they would both be learning together, Soren knew that now he must become the ryb, the teacher, the guide to this young owl who was king.

CHAPTER ONE

Grank I Am

Call me Grank. I am an old owl now as I set down these words but this story must be told, or at least begun before I pass on. Times are different now than they were when I was young. I was born into a time of chaos and everlasting wars. It was a time of magic and strange enchantments, a time of warring clans and warring kingdoms, a time of savagery and evil spirits, and worst of all, a time of hagsfiends. The days of old King H'rathmore, the High King of all of the N'yrthghar, were dark days, indeed. Lords and chieftains and petty princes raged against him and against one another, fracturing these kingdoms as surely as the summer breaks the frozen seas into the bergs and shards and floes of ice.

The lust for war carried from one generation to the next until there seemed no escaping it. When King H'rathmore died his young son, H'rath, then became High King. And I, being of noble birth, and dearest friend of King H'rath and his mate, Queen Siv, was drawn in deeper and deeper to this world of blood and battle, of intrigue and anarchy. It was not to my liking — unlike young King H'rath I was not the fiercest of soldiers. But I did serve him well as a confidant, and often as emissary to a restless clan or disaffected lord. I was, in truth, better with words than with the ice weapons with which the owls of the N'yrthghar fought. Better at planning strategy than rallying troops for battle. I had neither an affinity nor a temperament for this world of blood and battle, of intrigue and anarchy. And yet I felt duty bound to stay at my young king's side to help him unite his fractured kingdom, to resist and perhaps annihilate the hagsfiends and their insidious magic.

But even chaos has its rhythms and ongoing wars have their idle interludes, their moments of fragile peace. And it was during these times that I often ventured off by myself to explore matters far removed from those of war. You see, Good Owl, you must understand that even though H'rath, Siv, and I grew up the closest of friends and shared so much from the time before they became mates, I always was, and have remained, my own owl. I realized early on that I was one of those creatures destined to be alone, never to have a mate. The one owl whom I had desired, the one for whom my gizzard fairly sang was already . . . well, no need to talk of that now. I will simply say it was not to be.

CHAPTER TWO

I Discover Firesight

It was during the early part of H'rath's reign when a period of fragile peace had been achieved that I first took wing across the Sea of Kraka — or the Everwinter Sea as some called it — to that distant territory known as Beyond the Beyond. I wanted to see that fiery part of the world where it was said that the tops of mountains opened up like the mouths of enormous beasts and licked the sky with tongues of fire.

You see, fire had fascinated me from an early age. I saw things in fire that disturbed and intrigued me. And I found that for me to study fire was a way of steadying the gizzard and concentrating the mind. Whenever I suffered a dreariness of the gizzard I took quietly to the wing to lose myself in the sky I so cherished, and if I was lucky, to find when I looked down on the earth a fire, or a place to build one.

Almost immediately upon my first arrival in the Beyond, I felt my discontent ease. In the course of years, I would make many trips to the Beyond. And during those visits I enjoyed the hearty companionship of the dire wolves, the strange, loping creatures who had found their way to that fiery place some years before. I counted as a good friend their leader, the immense silvery wolf named Fengo. With Fengo by my side, I spent hours studying the eruptions of the volcanoes and, in particular, the trajectories of the embers that fell from the glowing fountains of fire. You must understand that at the time the world knew fire only for its destructive powers. In the kingdoms of N'yrthghar we did not even have a word for fire, for we lived in a nearly treeless place where lightning, when it struck, struck only rock or ice.

And so it was not through flame that I experienced my first visions. It happened on an early spring day. My parents had brought my sister and me out to learn the rudiments of First Flight. We were perched on a sloping expanse of ice on a part of the glacier popular for early lessons in takeoff and landing. The sun was quite fierce for that time of the year on the glacier. A shard of ice that stuck straight up from the ice beds had caught the sun, and the brightness was so dazzling that the air seemed to spin with a radiance I had never seen before. In the midst of this radiance, I began to see things. This struck me as odd, for owls are supposed to see best in darkness, but I was seeing beyond any darkness into a light that seemed to open up new realms of vision.

And what exactly did I see? Myself flying, doing everything my da had told us about lofting and ice hopping, and catching a breeze by tipping our primaries just so. The countless instructions came together within this vision and suddenly I knew in my gizzard how to fly. I lifted off the ground in one swift motion. My da and mum said they had never seen anything like it. My sister, Yurta, cried with envy. But oddly enough, I soon forgot about those visions over the long winter when the sun never rose above the horizon.

Forgot about them until I experienced my first forest fire. Only then did I remember what I had seen in the dancing radiance of the sun upon the ice. I was with my mother on an island in the Bitter Sea when a summer storm hit hard. A nearby tree was struck by lightning and burst into flame. My mother and I fled. I say fled but, in truth, I was almost transfixed by the fire. For it was in that sea of raging flames that I had what I have come to think of as my first true vision. It was a vision not of fire the destroyer but fire the creator. I saw not feathers being burned or animals screeching in terror, but owls pulling from the flames useful things that I had no names for, but which I knew could be put to good service. In the reflections of the sun on the ice shards, I had seen the present and the secrets of flight. But in the flames, it was as if I had glimpsed the future, or what might be. It was with this in mind that I set myself to the task of discovering the benefits, the blessings of fire. I intended to learn all I could and I was determined to capture an ember and with it explore how I might kindle a fire, and tame it as well.

Since forest fires were hard to come by in the N'yrthghar, I returned to the ice beds in a far corner of the Hrath'ghar glacier. It was spring once more, and the strength of the sun would be gaining every day through summer, which, though very short, was a radiant time of year. For the ice of the glacier never melted, and those reflections that had first ambushed me in a confusing crossfire of bouncing light when I was learning to fly did bear some resemblance to flames. I thought that they might help me delve deeper into my visions, this "magic" of seeing the present and, perhaps, the future and the past.

For me, it was a most wonderful spring and summer. Flying to that corner of the glacier was great fun as well. The katabats, those special winds of the N'yrthghar, were wonderfully boisterous that spring. I would sometimes go out of my way to ride the thermal drafts of the smee holes, those steam vents far to the east of the glacier near the Bay of Fangs, which offered a bouncing good flight. And the tiny beautiful flowers that dared to bloom at the edge of the avalanche and on the icy rim of the glacier delighted me. Their blossoms made gay the white and ice-bound world of the N'yrthghar. During those long, nearly nightless days of summer, illuminated by the tireless sun, I would immerse myself in the reflections bouncing off this dazzling whiteness. I wandered through radiant forests made of light shards and reflected beams; I found the bright shadows of all manner of creatures and friends, and the fleeting images of events, both past and future. I came to understand my visions more fully. For one thing, I understood that this was not a phenomenon that I could simply will to happen. The visions rarely came on demand. They came as they pleased and, perhaps, as I might best learn from them. But still they were not fire. They were not flame. They were merely shards of reflected light — never as clear and crisp as the images I had seen in the forest fire.

I began to think deeply about fire, and then one day, dancing in the sharp edges of that fractured light, I had a most intriguing vision — a patch of frost moss that appeared to smolder. Buried at its very center was a tiny glowing spark. I began to blow on it, which I quickly realized was ridiculous as it was only a vision and had no substance. But visions can be transformed into reality. I immediately flew out and gathered some of this frost moss and placed it on a pile of clear ice. I then found some pieces of loose ice and propped them up around the moss, in much the same manner as an ice nest is built, save for one difference: The pieces of ice faced the sun in such a way as to focus its rays on the moss. In essence, I had built a reflection chamber. It did not take long. Soon the patch of silvery-green moss was turning darker and then that scent that I had not smelled since the forest fire began to swirl through the air. I saw a spark of orange. My gizzard leaped! And then a flame. A true flame! I had made fire! The ice pieces were now melting and I quickly flung them away so that the water would not extinguish the tiny quivering flames that were just beginning.

Quite soon, I became adept at making these "moss fires," as I called them, and within the flames I found many visions, images that were far clearer and livelier than the ones borne by the sun's reflections. Thus, as I grew older, my visions enabled me to trespass the borders of time and fly into what I can only describe as another world, one that was not constrained by the movement of the sun across the sky, nor the phases of the moon. When I was experiencing visions, I was truly in a timeless universe.

But was this magic? I was not sure. There seemed to me to be a logic to the way this fire had ignited that was not at all magical. Yes, I did have powers of vision, but making fire from ice had been more the work of my gizzard and my brain than anything else. I felt I had discovered a connection not with magic but with certain laws of the natural world. In truth, I was relieved. I liked the notion of laws, for our N'yrthghar was a lawless place. I began to think that laws were in some way like trees, and without laws the winds swept through the N'yrthghar so fiercely that no owl could fly a true course. But it would be a very long time from these first moss fires until I would go to Beyond the Beyond to further my studies of fire.

Dear Owl, if, indeed, you are reading this book centuries from now, you probably do not know what a frightful power magic was in those days so long ago. You must first understand that in that time before time, there were fewer kinds of birds. In the most ancient of times, long before I had hatched, or even my great-great-grandparents had come into the world, there had been just one kind of songbird and one kind of seabird and one kind of bird of prey. After thousands upon thousands of years, the various species of birds separated and became distinct. There came to be robins and nightingales and larks, and so on and so forth. At one time, as unimaginable as it may seem now, there was a bird that was both crow and owl — a strange commingling of blood! Then gradually over many, many years these "crowls," as they were called, separated into distinct species. Yet, oddly enough, some never did. And these remnant crowls came to be known as hags-fiends. Their gizzards were different, warped, many said. And although they had somewhat primitive brains, these birds possessed strange inexplicable powers that could only be called magical. When I was growing up, it was still a time of great magic. And through my experiments and study of fire, I knew that I, too, possessed certain powers. I still had much to learn, and it was this thirst for knowledge that drew me to Beyond the Beyond — that land of erupting volcanoes — to study fire more closely. I wanted to learn how to fly the hot drafts that spiraled from the flames. I wanted to look into the gizzards of the hottest embers. For me, fire was alive. Fire had a body, an anatomy like any living thing.

CHAPTER THREE

Fengo

On my first visit to Beyond the Beyond during that peaceful lull in the wars of the N'yrthghar, I not only learned more about fire, but I learned about dire wolves, the immense creatures who had migrated to this region some years before. I remember as clearly as if it were yesterday when I first met Fengo, their chieftain. He had brought his clan to the Beyond when they could no longer endure what they called the Long Cold that had settled on their homeland. Fengo knew the terrain of the Beyond well and, most important, he knew the volcanoes. There were five volcanoes in what would later become known as the Sacred Ring. Fengo had an intimate knowledge of these volcanoes, their individual behaviors, the rhythms of their eruptions, the kinds of coals they spewed from their mouths.

When I first saw Fengo, he was perched on a high ridge. His incredible green eyes were fastened on a volcano on the north side of the ring. He did not say hello.

Nor did he scent mark immediately to warn me off or engage in any of the very complicated displays by which wolves signal their acceptance or rejection of any creature who is approaching. Furthermore, he gave no indication of his rank to suggest what honors were his due. No, there was none of that, which surprised me for I had met several wolves since I had been in the Beyond and they were quite touchy about such things. But here their chieftain, Fengo, remained perfectly still as I lighted down on the ridge not far from him. He did not look at me, but he spoke.

"Watch that one straight ahead on the north, right between the stars of the Great Fangs." He pointed with his muzzle to a volcano that was precisely centered between the lowest stars of the constellation that rose at this time of year. The constellation was identical to one that in the N'yrthghar we called the "Golden Talons."

"I am watching," I said.

"It is going to erupt when the last star of the Great Fangs rises above the horizon."

And so it did. I was astonished.

"How did you know that?"

"I know," was all he said.

He turned to me. The eyes of these dire wolves were a color I had never seen before. To say they were green does not do them justice. They were more like green fire. And Fengo's were absolutely astonishing. Our eyes locked and in that moment something passed between us. I knew then that although we were owl and wolf, two such different animals, we shared something: We both had visions. I could see the image of the volcanoes' flames reflected now in his eyes. As I peered deeper into that eerie greenness, I saw more. It was as if the eyes themselves were no longer eyes but something else. There was the reflection of orange flame, but in the center of that flame was a glimmer of blue and then a shimmer of green, the same green as the wolf's eyes. But I was not seeing eyes.

"You see it, don't you?" Fengo said.

"I see something but I am not sure what."

"It is an ember."

So it was in the eyes of the dire wolf Fengo that I caught my first glimpse of what would come to be known as the Ember of Hoole. I felt its power immediately. I sensed that it could be a dangerous thing to let loose in the world. But it also held the promise of great good.

"You came to learn about fire, did you not?" Fengo asked.

I nodded. I did not ask how he knew this. I understood that in many ways this wolf was like me. He was a flame reader. He had firesight. And he knew much, for he lived in a world of constant fire here in the Beyond.

"I can help you," he said. "I can teach you some things, but not everything. And you will soon learn more than I can teach, and know more than I can imagine."

This puzzled me. "How can that be?" I asked.

"You can fly," he said simply.

"But why should this help me learn more?"

"You are able to fly over the craters from which the fires leap. You can look into the heart of the volcano. On the wing, you shall catch the hottest coals."

"Catch coals?"

"Yes." Fengo nodded. "Catch coals and then make fire and see what can be made from fire. With that, I might be able to help you for I have explored the effects of flames on certain materials."

"It doesn't just burn things up?" I asked.

"Not always. Sometimes it changes things."

I was intrigued and was wondering what these changes could be when he interrupted my thoughts.

"And perhaps one day you shall see where the ember lies buried."

"Do you mean the wolf ember?" I asked him, for that was how I thought of the ember I had seen in his eyes.

"It is not the wolf ember," he said quietly. "It is the owl ember. Make no mistake. It is the Ember of Hoole."

"That cannot be!"

"Why not?"

"Because it has been told that Hoole was the first owl: In that time when all birds were alike, the first one to become an owl was called Hoole. It was even said that he was a mage. That he possessed good magic. But it is just a story from a time long ago when there were no high kings, no kings at all. The word 'Hoole' now means first of a kind.

"And in our wolf language the word 'Hoole' simply means owl. You see, my friend, it was the spirit of a Hoole that I followed when I led my kind here from our ice-locked land."

"The spirit of an owl? Not a real owl?" I asked him.

"Oh, she was real all right. But long dead."

"You mean a scroom, then."

"Yes, a scroom, if that is what you call the spirits of the dead."

"Hoole," I repeated the word softly. It had a lovely sound that seemed to spin out into the darkness like that wild and untamed song of the wolves when they howled into the night. "Hoole," I said it again. Like a silvery filament of moonlight, it whispered through the dark.

CHAPTER FOUR

BONK!

Although it had been only a reflection in Fengo's eyes, I became haunted by my brief vision of this ember. I sensed a power in this coal, power far beyond that of my visions, of being able to see the present in distant places where I was not flying or roosting, and events in a time that was not my own. On my subsequent trips, I flew over the five volcanoes countless times trying to figure out where the ember lay buried. It burned in my dreams, in my gizzard. Its power both fascinated and frightened me.

I learned much from Fengo at this time, much about fire and flame. He showed me how to start fires from the cooler embers that lay in the glowing coal beds that flanked the sides of the volcano. He showed me how nuggets of silver and gold could be melted by fire and shaped as they cooled. But more exciting to him than silver or gold were the rough rocks in which something he called the "deep metals" were locked. Fengo felt that there might be a way of extracting these metals if a hot enough fire could be built. But for that kind of fire, one had to retrieve coals before they hit they ground. They were the hottest of coals. Every time Fengo talked of this, his eyes gleamed.

"Grank, if we can make strong metal and learn how to shape things from it" — he paused — "well, it is almost unimaginable how our lives might change."

Fengo needed me to retrieve the coals, but I needed Fengo to craft the metals, for the wolf was amazingly skillful. With his teeth he gnawed intricate designs on the surface of bones. He often honed the edges of the bones into sharp objects, as sharp as any ice swords. And something similar to this and much more could be done with metal.

After this first trip, I returned to the Beyond several times over the years. Very few owls in the N'yrthghar knew about these journeys. When I was away, King H'rath and Queen Siv kept in touch with me by their most trusted messenger, Joss, who would bring me missives on the progress of peace, or its shattering, at which times I returned immediately.

I had learned much that I felt someday could be of benefit to H'rath and his kingdom, but catching a coal on the fly eluded me. I was feeling very frustrated by this inability, and one day was complaining bitterly to Fengo. "I don't understand it, Fengo. I have come this close so many times." I held up my talons and pinched the front two together. "And yet I always miss."

Fengo, who had been lying down, suddenly stood up and assumed a very erect stance. His tail was straight in a line with his spine and he stared hard at me and then growled. My gizzard lurched. Never in my long friendship with Fengo had he treated me like this. He was threatening me! His posture, his raised hackles, the stare, the growl were all the behaviors a low-ranking wolf could expect from a higher-ranking one. But why me? I am an owl. We were, in our own ways, equal.

"What is it?" I tried to look into his eyes, but I flinched. The ember blazed there as if his pupils were on fire. I had to look down. I dropped my head and, within a split second, I — an owl! — had slid into the posture and the gestures of a submissive, low-ranking wolf.

"You will never catch a coal until you put that one coal out of your mind: the ember of the owl."

"But it is called the owl ember. And I am an owl. It haunts me."

"It is not for you, this ember," he said. "At least, not now."

"Not now?" I waited for him to say more.

"You have learned much, Grank," he said finally. "But still not enough. If I had wings, I could fly those thermals better than you. You have been so obsessed by the one ember that you can't see the shapes of the wind. Heat carves wind, my friend. It sculpts it into bridges and air ladders and spires and mountains and tunnels and passageways. When you learn the windscapes of heated air, then you will know how to catch a coal on the fly."

Fengo was right. I had been a distracted student in this land of fire.

Fengo dropped his tail and his hackles lay flat. "Grank," he said softly, "think of all that you know about the ice and the winds coming off that ice in the N'yrthghar. There is not a katabat that you have not flown. You know that air, that wind of your country of the Great North Waters. Now you must learn about the heat and blazing winds of the Beyond."

And so I began that very night. The air surrounding and above a volcano is layered. There are strata in air just as I have seen in rock formations. And within these layers, there are distinct features, unique forms and particularities. I explored them all: every kind of thermal that each of the volcanoes created as it erupted, the strange columns of intensely heated air that soared, piling up marvelous thermal cushions. Between the top of the column and the bottom was a region rich in coals and embers of all sorts. The fire columns were different from the fire whirls that were spinning vortexes of heated air. "Hot tornadoes" I called them. Not nearly as rich in coals. I learned the structure of flame, its flanks, the pressure created in the air surrounding it. There were cool gaps that offered quick flight paths to slower-moving embers.

Every night I learned more and came closer and closer to catching a coal on the fly. I had been studying the shape of the wind for more than a moon cycle when one night toward dawn I was hovering in the bottom layer of a thermal cushion, my eyes scanning the fountain of coals that was bubbling at the top of the column. I could not go for them all. I knew I must focus on one, draw a bead on it. And so I did. In that moment, I was flooded with confidence. It was as if a pathway opened up leading directly to that coal. I plunged out of the thermal cushion and into the top of the column. My beak clamped down. It did not even burn. I had it!

"Bonk!" came a cry from below. It was Fengo howling for joy. I had no idea what this word "bonk" meant. Fengo leaped high into the air, his shaggy silver coat tinged orange in the reflected light of the fire and coals, and "bonk!" he howled again. When I asked him upon landing what the word meant, he said, "I don't know. It just came out." This was the way it was sometimes when one felt joy, the words just streamed out. Sometimes they made sense, other times they did not. We both laughed and from that day on we called these coals "bonk coals."

But I'll never forget that moment when I landed with the coal in my beak and dropped it in front of him. He stared down at the coal, which pulsed with a heat that stirred the air into shimmering waves. Once more he leaped high into the air, the moon silvering his pelt, and began to howl that savage untamed song of wolves in the night. He called to me as he shot higher and higher with each exuberant leap. "Grank, you are indeed a hunter of coals, a collier."

And so, though I had never before heard that word — collier — I knew what he said was right. I was indeed a collier. The *first* collier.

The finding of that bonk coal marked the beginning of a new phase of our education about fire. I was able to harvest a bountiful supply of coal, which provided us with a steady stream for our work. I learned not only how to fly those peculiar drafts of hot air but to follow the trajectories of the coals. I learned how to time their falls. We began building all sorts of fires and experimenting with rocks that bore traces of metal — and other things as well.

One night I had caught a small vole, and we decided just for the fun of it to try roasting the plump fellow. The burnt fur tasted awful but the meat was good, quite flavorful. So the next time I caught one, Fengo scraped off the fur so only the flesh was left. It was quite delicious. That was the beginning of all sorts of food experiments. But I have to say as flavorful as roasted meat was it went down rather dry. After a steady diet of it, I truly missed the blood.

Perhaps the most interesting experiments we tried with fire were those using sand. There was a particular kind of sand that could be found in the pits around the ring of volcanoes. When we heated it up to very a high temperature, curious transformations began. The bits of sand melted together and when it cooled became clear as the issen glossen or clear ice of the N'yrthghar. So we called it "glossen," or simply "gloss." Both of us were thrilled with this discovery, but for me, it also marked a strange interlude in my life. One for which I shall always feel deep shame. I cringe to think of it. But, Dear Owl, as a writer, I owe one thing to you, and that is complete honesty.

CHAPTER FIVE

A Strange Interlude

After our discovery of gloss, Joss arrived with a message calling me back to the N'yrthghar. War had not broken out nor had peace been shattered. I was called to attend the annual lemming hunt held by Lord Arrin, a powerful lord in the Firth of Fangs whose allegiance was vital to the High King.

Lord Arrin's realm was rich in issen blaue, a kind of ice that had many uses in the Northern Kingdoms, particularly for weapons. Also in the region of the Firth of Fangs, there was a preponderance of Great Snowy Owls who, as a breed, were particulary skillful fighters. Snowies were also known for their expertise in hunting lemmings; thus, the annual lemming hunt. So the Firth of Fangs was a region rich in resources vital to the High King. Add to this the additional fact that Lord Arrin himself was an owl of great vanity, and it would not do to offend him by not attending this event. I had secured for King H'rath the ice rights during the brief summer months when the issen blaue could be harvested. Each year these rights had to be renewed. It was always a delicate negotiation, and I was the chief negotiator.

So, as much as I hated to leave the Beyond, there was little choice. Too much was at stake. And, in truth, the lemming hunt was fun, for it was not all just chasing after those stupid rodents. There were festivities and katabat dancing, a particular specialty of owls of the Northern Kingdoms, in which we danced in those boisterous winds unique to our kingdom.

Lord Arrin was a generous host as well, and the bingle juice always flowed. There were always troops of gadfeathers to entertain us. Gadfeathers were wandering owls who were looked down upon in general, and often scorned by owls for having no solid place to roost. They lived for the most part by begging or stealing. But they were wonderful musicians and made a festive addition to any celebration. Festooning themselves in molted feathers from other birds, lacing moss and berries through their primaries, they were about as gaudy as an owl could get. Wonderful katabat dancers, they were a delight to watch and they were legendary for their singing. The gadfeathers sang all sorts of songs, merry ones to accompany a jig on a katabat, or achingly tender ballads of love and wandering. To hear a gadfeather's melodious voice singing a ballad under the starry arc of a lofty summer sky is an unmatched experience. Though I knew I would miss my fire studies, I felt little regret leaving the Beyond to go to Lord Arrin's lemming hunt in the Firth of Fangs.

When I finally returned to the Beyond after the lemming hunt, I had every hope that this would be an extended stay, for a fragile peace still reigned in the N'yrthghar. I had negotiated extended ice rights in the Firth of Fangs for King H'rath; at the same time, there was a sharp decline in hagsfiends' insurgencies, which Lord Arrin claimed credit for. All this boded well. Or so I thought.

Shortly after I had come back, I was flying over a volcano on the northwest side of the ring. This particular volcano had not been active for some time, and Fengo and I were thinking of moving one of our fires close to it as there were some good sand beds nearby, and sand was the main ingredient of gloss. I had not thought of the owl ember for a long time. I had truly cleared my mind of it. But as I was circling around this volcano, I saw a peculiar transformation taking place. It appeared as if the sides of the volcano were beginning to turn to gloss. I could see right through it. Was I having a vision? I knew that my firesight had become much keener since I had been coming to the Beyond, but this was very odd, not simply a vision. I was seeing something deep within the volcano itself. It was orange with a lick of blue at its center, circled with green. My gizzard flinched. It was the Ember of Hoole!

I forgot the sand beds I had come to examine, altered course, and flew directly over the crater. When I looked down, I saw a sea of boiling lava, but it suddenly grew still and calm. Then in a bubble of the lava on the surface, I spotted the ember rocking gently. It was as if it were beckoning to me. *Mine!* I thought. *Mine for the taking.* I began to fly up. I was looking for a cool gap, or a downdraft to power my spiraling plunge. I quickly found it, laid back my wings, and dived into the crater. I felt no heat. I felt nothing.

Within seconds I climbed the thermals back out of the crater and landed in a nearby sand pit. I was exhausted. Exhausted but exhilarated. I had the ember in my talons. The power of the thing seemed to surge through me. I don't know if I fell into a sleep or into some unconscious state, but when I awoke Fengo was standing over me.

"So you have it," he said drily. He did not sound joyful. Indeed, there was something dismal in his tone. But I ignored it. I would not let any creature mar this moment, tarnish my joy, my elation, my power. If I'd had powers before, they now felt magnified a thousand times over.

"Look," I said, "it continues to glow just as hot as when I first got it, even though it sits in sand and not fire."

"That is the nature of the ember," Fengo said. There was a dullness to his voice, a dullness tinged with regret. I could not stop staring at the ember. My obsession was not satisfied, my fascination not dimmed. I felt the ember's magic niggle into my gizzard and take hold of me. Thus, began my strange interlude. I still worked with Fengo to discover new things we could do with fire and rocks, fire and sand, and even fire and water. But we did not make much progress. It was not simply that my gizzard wasn't in it. It was as if I had slipped into a trance. The exposure to the ember had increased my firesight incredibly, but it seemed I could not act upon what I saw. It did not move me.

And here is what I saw, beginning with my first glimpse into the coal. I know not how long this vision went on, for once more I had entered a timeless place.

I saw one of King H'rath's most skillful ice harvesters, a Burrowing Owl named H'rooth, suddenly plummet in flight. I saw a hagsfiend slice off his head, raise it on an ice blade, and fly off into the dark sky with blood streaming through the night air like a wild river, turning the stars and the moon red. I saw other ice harvesters falling, their severed heads caught on the sharp points of curved ice scythes, the kind always carried by hagsfiends. And the hagsfiends flying off screeching, with gruesome trophies of murder, their ragged dark wings blacker than any night.

What could this mean? I had thought the hagsfiends had retreated, particularly from the Firth of Fangs where Lord Arrin claimed to have put down their insurrections so successfully. But then it all suddenly became clear to me: I saw Pleek, a Great Horned Owl, long an enemy of Hrath's and known to consort with hagsfiends. Indeed, it was rumored that Pleek had taken one as a mate. Her name was Ygryk. In the ember, I saw them flying with Lord Arrin's knights.

It was unthinkable that Lord Arrin, the chieftain I had so recently visited, was attacking King H'rath's ice harvesters, the very ice harvesters for whom I had negotiated ice rights. Had it all been a trick to lure these owls into Lord Arrin's realm so he could kill them and thus deprive the High King of weapons and able knights? I saw all of this but I was not moved. I felt no alarm, not even the mildest stirring of my gizzard. It did not touch me. I did nothing. I saw Lord Arrin's troops of vassals, knights, and even hireclaws massing on a northern point of the Firth of Fangs with Pleek's fiercest lieutenants leading them. I saw Lord Arrin himself dispatching hagsfiend scouts in the direction of the Hrath'ghar ridge. And this could mean only one thing. Invasion.

For all my ability to see the treachery of Lord Arrin in the present and to glimpse the disasters in the near future, I did nothing. I was suspended in a kind of void. When I was not looking into the flames of the fires that Fengo and I built, I was staring into the ember. This went on for some time. I knew deep in my gizzard that my inaction meant disaster for my two closest friends, King H'rath and Queen Siv, and still I did nothing.

For nights and nights, moon cycle after moon cycle, I remained in that peculiar numb state. In truth, I was no longer a creature of time. For all my powers, I was not aware of its passage. I drifted apart from Fengo. Or perhaps he left me out of boredom and disgust. I heard him sneer one day when I had become too lazy to try a new rock in the fire, "Go on, go stare at the ember." He would never say "your ember." It was always just "the ember." This alone should have given me a hint.

Then one night, Joss came with a message from the N'yrthghar. He arrived, breathing hard, his feathers shredded on their leading edges from the harsh weather that had set in.

"It's a message from your king!" Fengo growled. I continued to stare into the ember. "Your king is calling you, Grank."

"What's wrong with him?" Joss asked, staring at me.

Fengo did not answer him but walked up between the ember and me. He butted me with his head, then pointed his tail straight out and the hackles on the back of his neck stood erect. He was threatening me again. Humiliating me in front of a servant of the king. For me, the king's closest advisor, to be treated this way was unthinkable. But did I care? Not really.

Joss gave me the message scrawled on a piece of lemming hide. Few owls read, so there was very little danger of anyone understanding the message if Joss had been captured, but still I was warned to "burn this missive after you finish reading it, burn it in those fires you are always studying." The message was from H'rath, my king and friend. It began:

"These are most grievous times. I sense a deep and devious plot against me. My ice harvesters have not returned from their expedition to the Firth of Fangs. I do not know whom to trust. I fear that some of my oldest allies have joined ranks with hagsfiends. Fragile coalitions with neighboring clans are disintegrating. They all lust for nachtmagen."

Ha! I almost laughed out loud. Nachtmagen! Hagsfiends' magic could not compare to mine. It is astonishing that it did not occur to me even then that I had done nothing with my new power except to gaze deeper into the ember to see more and more terrible things. I read on:

"Siv has set an egg."

I felt a twinge in my gizzard for the first time in a long while.

"Promise me, dear Grank, that if something happens to me, you shall protect my family. Protect Siv, her egg, and when the time comes, the hatchling. But now you must come home. We need you desperately. Should anything happen to me —" The writing broke off. Something must have interrupted him. I dimly remembered seeing something in the fire earlier in the evening — a flood of hagsfiends sweeping down off the ice fortress of Hrath'ghar ridge. Blood.

I took the thin piece of hide and dropped it into the fire. I watched the flames. Yes, a battle was raging. It did not look good for the H'rathian troops. I yawned. I saw Joss look around the camp. It was littered with my yarped pellets. I was living in squalor. I blinked. Then I looked at Joss. "I know all this that is in the message."

"You do?" Joss said, shocked. "Then why have you not come?"

"I don't know," I replied blandly.

Fengo stepped close to me. "Return the ember to the volcano, Grank. It is not for you. Its magic is too strong. You are a good owl, perhaps a mage, but you are not powerful enough to bear exposure to the ember."

I blinked. "I don't understand."

"It is too strong for you and it is too dangerous to chance it falling into the possession of a hagsfiend or an evil owl."

"Would it not be too strong for them, too?" I asked.

"Yes, but they would use it. And it would magnify their evilness, their nachtmagen. But if by chance a good owl, a noble owl of great grace and great strength would find it, the ember would not be too strong, and he or she would use the magic for the good of all owlkind. You are good, dear friend, but you are not that owl."

"Then who am I?" I said in a frail voice, and looked around. For just then I seemed to realize I had somehow mislaid my very self.

"You will find yourself when you put the ember back."

"Put it back?"

"Fly back to the volcano, Grank. Drop the ember into the crater and let it lie buried until an owl is hatched who will use it well."

And so I did. I felt the power of the ember slip from me the moment I dropped it into that bubbling cauldron of lava. I felt my gizzard expand and realized that for many long days and nights it had been pinched and hard. I felt my self, my real self, seep back. My gizzard quickened. I was ready. The volcano had erupted. The flames scoured the night, turning the moon and the stars crimson. And in those flames I saw terrible things. Things that I had ignored too long. I knew that I must fly back to the N'yrthghar as quickly as possible.

CHAPTER SIX

When We Were Very Young

It was the season of the N'yrthnookah, which meant that the winds were on the beak. It would be a long trip back, a tough claw-flight. I would have to fly off the wind and claw against the easterly current to keep from being set too far west. The trees grew thickly in the Shadow Forest, so I flew low between them where I would gain some protection from the wind.

I was flooded with memories of H'rath and Siv as I flew back to the N'yrthghar. The three of us had known one another since we were mere hatchlings skidding about on the glaciers, not yet able to fly. We were all of noble birth: H'rath a prince, son of the High King, Siv the daughter of a chieftain, and I myself a prince, though my father was not a High King. It was obvious from the start that H'rath was born to rule. I, however, was not. Nor did I have any desire to become a king or a chieftain. I was of a studious nature, and I realized that I could best serve owlkind not as a chieftain or a warrior but as an advisor. I sensed from the time that I had my first vision that this strange sight of mine would separate me from others, that it would be as much a burden as a gift.

It did not take long before word of my visions got around. My parents had been proud that I had learned how to fly so quickly and, as all proud parents, they bragged a bit, talked about how I had seemed to see "sun-spots with pictures" was how they put it. I soon felt other young owls in nearby ice hollows withdrawing from me. All except for H'rath and Siv. As soon as we learned how to fly we became inseparable, the three of us. I loved Siv from the start, but I could see that I was no match for H'rath. He was a big handsome Spotted Owl, always joking, but with a fine spirit and, yes, a natural talent for leadership.

Still, I tried my best to keep my visions to myself and did not discuss them even with my two closest friends. Sometimes, however, I could not stay silent. And once my vision saved H'rath's life.

We were still quite young and had been gleeking about on the spring drafts that rake the cliffs of the Hrath'ghar mountains. It was great fun and we were doing all sorts of acrobatic flight tricks. The three of us loved showing off for one another. We made up names for our different moves. There was the kukla spiral, "kukla" being the word in Krakish for crazy. There was the hag's swirl, but if anyone knew we had used that word — or even part of that word — in jest, we would have had our ear slits boxed. And then there was dizzy-izzy, which was quite comical looking. We would rotate our tails in one direction and then tilt our primaries into the wind and go spinning up and up and up until we could go no higher, often yarping up what we had just eaten. We had just finished a spectacular set of dizzy-izzies when we heard a call from a nearby ice shelf.

"Some flying!" a Great Gray Owl called to us. He was perched on the shelf and was picking over a lemming he had just caught.

"He's a warrior," Siv whispered. She could tell from the long blood-streaked ice shard at his side.

"He must be returning from the campaigns in the south!" H'rath said, his voice absolutely bursting with excitement. H'rath loved warriors. He dreamed of ice shards and ice swords and all the weapons that the owls of the north fought with.

"Come on over. This is a fat lemming, plenty for everyone."

We, of course, flew over. If he was in this part of the Hrath'ghar glacier, he was not an enemy. The enemy in those days was in the southern and eastern parts of the

N'yrthghar Kingdom. And Hrath'ghar was the stronghold of the H'rathians, followers of King H'rathmore, H'rath's father. So we flew over and settled on the shelf.

H'rath eyes were immediately drawn to the ice sword. "It still has blood on it," he said with wonder in his voice.

"Course it does. Blood of a Screech Owl, one of Hengen's knights."

"Hengen, Hag of Mylotte?" H'rath asked.

"Indeed, young'un," the Great Gray answered.

Hengen, Hag of Mylotte, was one of the most savage knight warriors of a chieftain who had allied himself with Mylotte, a powerful hagsfiend. While H'rath was looking at the ice sword, I was looking at the lemming. It was plump and succulent and its fur glistened in the pale twilight of this late winter day. I could feel my gizzard rumble with hunger.

"Let your prince eat first," said the Great Gray. I grew very still. I felt my eyes blur as they often did right before a vision came, but this time, there was no fire and no sunlight. I was standing very still. "Eat up, lad!" the Great Gray was saying.

"No," I said.

"What's wrong? It's a perfectly good lemming," the owl replied, a nasty edge to his voice. But when I stared at the lemming, I saw something green coiled within it.

"No!" I shrieked this time, and with my talons kicked the lemming off the edge of the ice shelf. A terrible hiss scalded the air as a bright eerie green thing slithered through the gathering darkness.

"A flying snake!" H'rath shouted, and we backed ourselves against the wall of the ice shelf. The snake coiled at once as if to strike.

I rose straight up into the air. And although I scarcely remembered it later, I was told that I spoke in strange words and at once the snake appeared to go yeep but then turned and glided off into the night.

The Great Gray was gone by the time we recovered.

"He tried to kill us!" H'rath said in stunned disbelief.

"He tried to kill *you*," Siv said.

"You're right," H'rath said. "He said that the prince should eat first."

And we all knew which prince he meant. At that moment they both turned to me. "Grank," H'rath whispered. "You saved my life. How did you know?"

"I'm not sure. I just see things sometimes."

"But never quite like this!" Siv said.

She was right. Never quite like this.

"Yes," I said softly. "Never quite like this." For I, too, was mystified.

"Grank," Siv said again, and stepped toward me, her lovely amber eyes glistening. "Are you a mage?" This sent a tremor through me, as well it should have.

How exactly does the magic of a mage differ from a hagsfiend's magic? When I was young, there was really only one kind of magic, nachtmagen, or bad magic, the magic of hagsfiends. But it was rumored that there were mages who practiced good magic. Some said the owl we called Hoole had been a mage. But most owls thought that this was pure invention. Good magic was something longed for but few believed it truly existed. I was not sure what had happened to me in that instant when I had lofted into the air and spoken those unintelligible words to the snake. When I came back down onto the ice shelf to face Siv's questions I was in a daze. I tried to reply honestly.

"I don't know. I don't know what happened. It was not like firesight at all. It was much more. But if I have magic . . ."

In that instant I saw them both wilf. They seemed to shrink, and their feathers lay close to their sides.

"Please," I begged, "don't be frightened of me. If you fear me I shall have no one." I could too easily imagine my friends making the sign with their talons to avert the evil eye when I came near, as was the custom if one was suspected of having magical powers.

It was at that moment that Siv stepped forward. "Never, Grank. We shall always be your friends." H'rath, too, came close and touched my wing with his talon.

"Always," he said. "And we shall speak nothing of these powers of yours. We promise." And then on that same ice shelf, where the sword, which was supposedly stained with the blood of Hengen, had lain, both Siv and H'rath struck off an ice splinter and pricked the meatiest part of their talons and pressed them together. It was a blood oath.

"I, H'rath . . ."

"And I, Siv . . ."

"Do hereby swear," they spoke in unison, "never to reveal what happened on this ice shelf, and to keep to ourselves the powers that our dearest friend, Grank, possesses. By Glaux, we swear this blood oath."

I was deeply touched. There was a slight shiver in my gizzard. I blinked and felt myself rich to have such friends. But yet again I had that awful feeling of being separate. Their loyalty was unquestionable, but as I perched on that shelf of ice watching these two wonderful young owls, I realized that they would always be together and I would always have to be apart. And yet, I thought, perhaps the sum of us would be great.

I had many questions about what the three of us had experienced on that ice shelf in the twilight. Was the warrior indeed a hagsfiend in disguise? It was said that hagsfiends, very powerful ones, could change their appearance. Become more owl than crow, but that even in disguise they still carried the lingering scent of crow.

After that encounter with the warrior and his evil designs, my explorations into a deeper understanding of my visions would begin in earnest. I wanted to know what good magic was and how it differed from the magic of hagsfiends. They were creatures of rage and malice in a lawless time. If there was such a thing as good magic could the hagsfiends be countered? Or did any use of magic lead one into an unholy alliance with evil? There was at that time a small group of owls — called the Glauxian Brothers — who believed that hagsfiends existed because owlkind had somehow lost its faith in Glaux, and in reason. They believed that this loss of faith and reason had created a tear, a rip in the very air of the owl universe, and it was through this tear that these creatures of rage and superstition and nachtmagen had entered our world. I worried, too, what would happen to me if other owls discovered I had these powers. I began to think very hard about the lemming with the venomous snake embedded in its body. How had I been able to see that? There had to be some connection between my firesight and this magic, my vision and the enchantment I had mysteriously cast to make the snake flee. All these long-ago memories swirled through my head as I flew back to the N'yrthghar, at the behest of H'rath, my friend and king.

Back to the N'rythghar, where hagsfiends were once more on the rise. How odd that such a short time ago I had attended the lemming hunt and negotiated so skillfully with Lord Arrin. What had transpired in the meantime? What haggish bargain had the vain lord made with the fiends? And would it spread like some disease? For if all the deceitful lords and rebellious princes and rancorous chieftains began to join with the hagsfiends, would it not spell the end of owlkind as we knew it? Would time wind back to that most ancient of all eras, the time of the crowls? Would these remnant birds ascend and rule the world of owls? Nachtmagen would reign and chaos would shake the air, the winds, the clouds, the very foundations of the sky.

CHAPTER SEVEN

The Grog Tree

It was tiring winding in and out of the timber trying to shelter myself from the adverse winds. When I reached the border between the Shadow Forest and Silverveil, I stopped at a grog tree for some refreshment.

It was a rowdy scene indeed, with hireclaws back from the wars in the N'yrthghar. Some were well beyond tipsy, and many of them were flat-out trufynkken on the juice of the strong berries. I stopped not only to refresh myself but also to pick up information. One couldn't do better than a grog tree for finding out the latest news, gossip, and stories of the owl kingdoms. Before I came even close to the tree, I was careful to stash the few coals that I had brought back in a clever sling that Fengo had fashioned for me from the horn and sinew of a moose that he and some of his clan had brought down. It was perfect for carrying coals, being completely fireproof. I didn't want anybody getting too curious about where I had been or where I was heading.

Of course, that was the first question I encountered. A trufynkken Great Gray tumbled off a branch and nearly whacked me on the head. A huge belch ripped from him and then he yarped the most enormous pellet I had ever seen.

"Oh, what a prince you are!" a voice exclaimed behind me.

I nearly took straight off. The last thing I wanted anyone to know was my true identity. But I quickly realized that the owl who said this was referring to the Great Gray.

"Sorry, mate." The Great Gray dipped his head in apology and then fell flat on his beak.

"Out cold, the old sot." It was a rather pretty Barred Owl who had spoken. "Lovely, ain't he?" She looked at me, her amber eyes a bit bleary with grog.

"Now, what be your name, handsome, and where be you heading?"

I had no intention of giving an accurate answer. "Falen," I answered, with the first name that popped into my head. If I had said Grank or Ragfir, Ifghar or Brakvik, or any one of our harsh names in which sounds grind up against one another, it would have been a dead giveaway that I was from the N'yrthghar. "And I am going toward the desert," I told her.

"Oh, now, what do you want to go there for, lovey? No

44

trees, bunch of low-class owls? Why, you know them owls, they dig holes in the dirt and live in them!"

Now, Good Owl, perhaps you have already guessed that this Barred Owl, whose name turned out to be Maisy, was not of noble origins herself, and hardly what one might call a high-class owl.

"Come share a cup with me, lovey," she said.

The last thing Maisy needed was another cup of the berry brew. We hopped upon the trunk of a fallen tree. A one-eyed Great Horned was setting out chestnut cups filled with a mash of berries and juice. "What'll it be, Maisy?" By this time, Maisy was leaning hard against my port wing. "The usual." She hiccuped softly. "Sorry," she said to me with what I am sure she thought was a coquettish giggle. She tried snuggling up closer to me but fell over. She picked herself up and muffled a burp. The Great Horned winked his one eye at me.

Another Screech Owl came up to the trunk. He had a nasty gash on his starboard talon. I could tell immediately that it was a wound made by an ice dagger.

"Back from the north wars, eh, Flynn?" the Great Horned asked.

"Yeah, and I got this to prove it!" He held up the wounded talon.

"Hope you got more than that."

"Aye, they pay well, them norther owls."

"Where were you fighting?"

"Up in the Firth of Fangs," he answered.

"Any fighting up on the glacier?" I asked.

"Oh, yeah. A lot."

"How's the king doing?" I asked.

He shook his head. "Don't know what to believe. Some say he's dead. Others say he and the queen have fled. They say she done laid an egg. That there be an heir on the way and they be 'fraid the hagsfiends will get it."

"Dead? Dead, you say?" I demanded of him.

"I don't say. But it's what I hear."

I wondered how I had not seen this in the ember. Perhaps it wasn't true. A Burrowing Owl who had been listening now interrupted. "Oh, the High King is dead, all right. I seen it," the stranger said.

"You saw it? How's that?" I asked, trying to mask my emotions.

"I come up to fight for the king," the stranger went on. "You see, me brother was an ice harvester. He done got killed by them hagsfiends that Lord Arrin mustered for the first attacks a while back. I came to fight my brother's murderers. So I was there at the last battle of the king. I seen what they did to him. Lord Arrin got him cornered, all right, but it was them hagsfiends that finished him, the one called Penryck gave the final . . ." He hesitated, then lowered his voice. "You know what they do, sir, don't you?"

"Yes," I replied weakly. I knew Penryck. He was a hideous hagsfiend with extremely long tail feathers that stropped the air like razor ice. That and a crest of spiky tufts that grew along his spine gave him an almost reptilian appearance. Indeed, some called him Sklardrog, which in Krakish means "sky dragon."

"I saw the King's head on the scythe. Yes, sir, I did, indeed. On Penryck's scythe. I believe the lady, good Queen Siv, saw it, too."

"Oh, my Glaux!" I gasped. The very thought of Siv seeing this grisly spectacle made my gizzard lock. The stranger went on to give details, which I was too stunned to take in but would remember later.

And it was too easy to imagine Siv now, the most beautiful Spotted Owl in the world, desperate, possibly alone, and terrified that her first egg, the egg of H'rath and herself, would be seized, or worse, destroyed. I had to get flying. I started to move away from the grog tree.

"Oh, darlin'." Maisy tipped over and lay with her head on the trunk. "Where you be goin'?"

"The desert, remember?"

"Need company?" she asked.

"I thought you didn't like the desert. Full of low-class types. Remember?"

"Did I say that?" Her eyes blinked shut for a long time. And I was already moving off.

As I spiraled up and over the Shadow Forest, clawing against that hard northeasterly wind, I tried to think where Siv would have fled to in the N'yrthghar. Would she have gone farther north and west, deep into the range of the Hrath'ghar mountains? But if troops had been massing on that ridge, as I had seen in the flames, the way might be blocked. Perhaps she had flown straight west toward the Bitter Sea or the Bay of Kiel. Then I remembered that Siv had a cousin who had decided to begin a spiritual order, like that of the Glauxian Brothers, on the Island of Elsemere. Surely that would be a safe haven for Siv and her egg.

What I did not know, Dear Owl, and would not learn until later was that at the same time I was flying, clawing my way against that haggish wind toward the Glauxian Sisters Retreat, Siv was hiding from them. Indeed, the unthinkable had transpired! The retreat of the Glauxian

Sisters had been infiltrated by hagsfiends, and these fiends had used their most evil magic to cast a peculiar spell on the pious sisters of Glaux. It had been Myrrthe, Siv's faithful servant, an elderly but still-keen Snowy Owl, who had sensed that something was deeply amiss.

CHAPTER EIGHT
The Nacht Ga'

"Begging your pardon, madam," the old Snowy Owl said. "But could you offer some refuge to a poor gadfeather who has worn her plummels to a fray and has not tasted a decent lemming in the half cycle of the moon?"

Both Myrrthe and Siv had disguised themselves, weaving bits of moss, winter berries, and dried flowers through their feathers, imitating the gaudily adorned plumage distinctive of gadfeathers. Myrrthe mimicked, as well, the singsongy voices of these birds. The disguise had served them well but the two had decided it was best if Myrtthe went alone to Elsemere to make sure Siv's cousin, the mother superior, was still there. Some years before, Siv and Myrrthe had spent a delightful summer visiting with Siv's cousin and the sisters.

The mother superior, or Glauxess, of the order quickly glanced at the old Snowy who appeared at the entry to the underground burrow. She nodded and welcomed her.

"Why, of course," the Glauxess answered. "You are welcome here."

Myrrthe regarded her closely. She looked like Siv's cousin Rorkna but seemed changed in some way Myrrthe could not quite pinpoint. She immediately became wary. Following Rorkna, the mother superior, Myrrthe wound her way through the tunnels that connected the burrows of the retreat. They arrived at a larger burrow, where a pile of plump voles lay. The sight of food made Myrrthe's gizzard growl.

"What be your name, ma'am?" the Glauxess asked.

Myrrthe felt her gizzard lock. What be your name? This was poorly spoken Krakish. No one of royal or noble gizzard would ever speak this way. Myrrthe fought the instinct to wilf. She must not betray her suspicions, her fears. She would eat the vole quietly and then leave as fast as she could. She thanked Glaux that she had insisted that Siv remain tucked in at the base of the Ice Dagger, a short flight away. She suspected what might be going on here. If it was true, then the evil intricacies of the hagsfiends' nachtmagen was worse than she had ever imagined. Myrrthe had heard stories from an old aunt that there was a spell that some very powerful hagsfiends could cast, called the Nacht Ga'. But her auntie had been a nervous, apprehensive type, imagining a hagsfiend around every corner and making the slashing sign with her talon to ward off evil. So Myrrthe had never given much credence to her ramblings about hagsfiends and nachtmagen. But now Myrrthe's gizzard gave an alarming twitch.

Let me explain something, Dear Owl, about the nature of the gizzard. The gizzard is not simply a second stomach that accommodates the indigestible parts of our prey by compressing bones and fur and teeth into neat little pellets. Hardly! It is through this most mysterious of all organs that we experience our strongest feelings, emotions, and instincts. But it is more even than that. The gizzard of an owl can possess or develop what we call "Ga'," which means great spirit; a spirit that somehow embodies not only all that is noble, but all that is humble as well. It flourishes, however, to its greatest in very few owls. H'rath, for example, was a kind and great king. But did he have great Ga'? It is a hard question to answer. At that time in my life, I had never met an owl who could be said to have great Ga'. The extent to which Ga' evolves within an owl varies. But the seeds of it are there in every owl.

The spell of the hagsfiends, the Nacht Ga', freezes the seeds of a gizzard's Ga'; in fact, the spell suppresses all of the rare and extraordinary powers of the gizzard, turning that marvelous organ into what it was in the most common of birds — a mere second stomach, a lump in the gut. The spell allows the hagsfiends to invade an owl's being and force that bird to do their bidding. Although the owl might look as it did before, the owl's gizzard, its identity, the very essence of its owlness and personality were now in thrall to other powers — those of the hagsfiends. So even though the Glauxess looked exactly as she had before, she was not. She had been rendered powerless to exercise any moral judgment, powerless to act upon any conviction, powerless even to think any genuine thoughts.

Myrrthe now knew that Rorkna and the other sisters had fallen under this spell. Even if she had not known about the Nacht Ga', she would have wondered about the strange grinding noises coming from their gizzards. She knew the cause was not a bad vole — mere indigestion. The old Snowy knew that she must get away from this place as quickly as possible. She looked at the rock slab in the large burrow where she and the others shared the vole. Dread swept through her: She was not surrounded by the good sisters of Glaux but by hagsfiends who merely looked like the sisters. One false move and they would be on her like a pack of mobbing crows. She had to exercise the utmost caution. Her gizzard contracted and trembled as Rorkna spoke.

"Would you not honor us with one of your ancient gadfeather songs?"

Ancient gadfeather songs! Myrrthe thought frantically. Did she know any ancient gadfeather songs? Something sounded dimly in her brain. "Yes," she said hesitatingly. "Let me just get these vole teeth set away in my gizzard." She gulped and pretended to be flexing her gizzard, which, in truth, was trembling so hard it was barely functional. She was trying to buy herself some time. She then coughed delicately. The words of the song were coming back, and she sang:

> *From a time before time*
> *when we gadfeathers roamed*
> *o'er mountains, valleys, and sea,*
> *We sought not a home,*
> *not a limb for a perch,*
> *we only wanted to be free.*
>
> *Now the sky is our hollow,*
> *the stars we do follow.*
> *The wind is our friend.*
> *That's all we need in the end;*
> *To fly and rarely rest.*

The whole world is our nest.
Let us be, let us be, let us be.
Let us be free, free, free!

"Lovely! Ain't it, Sisters?" the Glauxess turned and spoke to the others.

The word "ain't" ground in Myrrthe's ear slits as loudly as the gizzards grinding around her. She could not leave quickly enough. As soon as she could, she bade the spellbound sisters farewell.

Taking her leave, Myrrthe set off on a roundabout flight path for fear of being followed, and finally returned to Siv, who awaited her in a crevice at the base of the Ice Dagger. Siv was sitting on the sling in which she carried the egg.

"Well?" Siv asked eagerly. "What took you so long?"

"Bad news, milady," Myrrthe replied.

"Rorkna hasn't died, has she?"

"Worse, actually."

Siv felt her gizzard flinch. "Worse! What do you mean?"

"Rorkna and all the sisters are spellbound. The Nacht Ga'."

Myrrthe thought that Siv might faint. Her sparkling eyes became lusterless. She swayed on her perch over the egg.

How Myrrthe wished she had a crop, one of those gullet pouches that other birds had. Then she could have brought up some of that vole to feed her lady. "There, there, milady," she said.

Siv staggered a bit, then steading herself atop the egg. "Don't worry, Myrrthe. I shall be fine. But I suppose we must leave here soon."

"Yes, milady. As soon as possible. Weather is coming in."

"Thank Glaux, you fashioned this fine sling for the dear egg."

"Yes, well, snow mice are more than just good to eat. Their pelts are useful, too. Madam?"

"Yes, Myrrthe?"

Myrrthe peeked out of the crevice. Snow was coming down harder. "I think we should go right now — by day. It's starting to really blizzard. So I'll blend in fine. Once I get rid of all these gadfeather trappings."

"Yes," Siv agreed. "Time to get rid of these gaudy accessories. Odd, though, isn't it? My great-aunt who was never even close to being a gadfeather loved all these trimmings. In moderation, of course. Still, I think spots are accessories enough for Spotted Owls. I shall begin to spottilate right now and this should obscure most of my darker feathers."

Myrrthe nodded.

Spottilating was a very clever trick that Siv, H'rath, and I had devised for camouflage flights in blizzards. It involved fluffing the feathers in a certain way so that the white spots that mottled our darker plumage spread to cover the brown, thus making us appear whiter.

This trick never ceased to amaze Myrrthe, and she watched in silence as Siv slowly became an almost pure-white owl. Then they rose off the Ice Dagger and within mere seconds melted into the white rage of the blizzard.

CHAPTER NINE
The Eyes of Fengo

In the whiteness of that blizzard, another owl had spot-tilated as well. Myself. And so we passed each other without ever knowing it. Aah! So clever we were. Ha! White fools flying through a white night! I bound for Elsemere, and Siv and Myrrthe just lifting off from the Ice Dagger upon which I would land in minutes to rest before pressing on to the sisters' retreat. I lighted upon the Dagger and almost immediately saw signs that owls had been here. I examined their talon prints closely. I felt my gizzard quicken and then it nearly shimmered when I spotted a feather. It was Siv's. I knew it. It just had to be. I was almost certain that she was a short flight away on the Island of Elsemere.

I was so excited that as soon as I regained my strength I lifted off and set a course for Elsemere through the blinding blizzard. I had always had very keen white vision, something that owls of the N'yrthghar came by naturally because of our long winters, but my white vision was especially sharp now. So the scratchy outline of the island soon appeared out of the blizzard, but at nearly the same time, my gizzard gave a lurch that nearly sent me into an air tumble. I began backwinging immediately. I didn't need to gaze into a fire to know that there was something awful happening to the sisters of Glaux on the Island of Elsemere. I suddenly realized that my powers of intuition had been intensified. This new power must have come about because of my exposure to the ember. Now I knew what I must do.

I began to circle back to the Ice Dagger. Thank Glaux, I had brought the horn with the coals in it. I would build a fire to see more precisely what was transpiring on Elsemere with the sisters and possibly Siv. And this time I would act. No, I would not fall prey to that dazed, hypnotic state in which I saw everything but did nothing.

Using some moss and small twigs I always carried in a lemming-skin pouch, I soon had a small but very serviceable fire going. I squatted down on the windward side of it so the flames would not blow in my face and began to read them. First, I scanned the licks of orange-and-yellow flames for any sign of Siv but could find nothing. I quickly realized that this was rather stupid of me. Hadn't I learned after all these years that the images from the fire could not be hunted down? I would not find them; they would find me. As soon as I relaxed and stepped back a pace from the fire, things became much clearer. And what I saw truly terrified me.

There was a Nacht Ga' cast upon the sisters of the island. It bound them and their gizzards as tightly as if they were trapped between two crunching ice floes. But there was no sign of Siv. Yet instinctively I felt she must be nearby. I had found feather traces of her here. And it was only reasonable that she would have gone to visit her dear cousin at this desperate time. My problem was trying to reason at all. I was caught between the evil magic of the hagsfiends and my own powerful magic. Reason is not a fulcrum for magic upon which decisions should be made. Nor is magic a fulcrum for reason. To mix logic with magic can be catastrophic. I was about to find this out.

I smothered the fire and thought. Reason commanded that I must go to Elsemere because, logically, Siv must be there, even though she was not brought forward by the flames. I knew that flames had their limitations. I also knew that the Nacht Ga' must be broken, whether Siv was there or not. It was sheer brutality to have enslaved the gizzards of these good sisters in such a manner. I must save them. There was only one way in which a Nacht Ga' spell could be broken and that was with a splinter made of issen blaue, which is the hardest of what we call the "strong ice." Normally, a single stab with one of these ice splinters was instantly fatal, but in the peculiar case of a spellbound owl, the wound broke the spell and restored the owl's gizzard.

Some of the very best ice splinters could be struck off the Ice Dagger itself. The Ice Dagger was a blade of rock soaring from the sea and sheathed in ice. One of the first lessons in our youth was to learn ice knapping. Old King H'rathmore sent us with his master-at-arms, Proudfoot, a Snowy, to this very Ice Dagger where we learned the craft of making weapons from ice. We learned how to use stones and various kinds of ice shards to strike off other pieces of ice and to fashion them into weapons. It was a craft known only in the N'yrthghar and it demanded real skill. Both H'rath and I became fairly good ice knappers.

I now made three sliver swords. They were minuscule. I carefully wrapped them in protective layers of moss so I would not cut myself and tucked them close to my shoulder between by my coverts and my flight feathers.

I circled Elsemere Island twice before lighting down on its eastern shore. An elderly sister, a hunched Barred Owl, waddled out of a burrow hole near one of the few trees and approached me. I knew immediately that what I had suspected was true. She was in the grip of the Nacht Ga.' Her normally warm brown eyes were dull, and there was a hint of that intense yellow behind them that is the mark of all hagsfiends.

"How may I serve you, good sir?" Her voice was mechanical, without the usual low melodious tones of a Barred Owl's speech.

"Just need a bit of a rest," I replied.

"A bit of vole might do you some good," she said.

"That would be very kind of you, madam."

"Follow me, then."

I followed her into a burrow opening, one of many that were scattered across the island, and soon found myself wending my way behind her through the twisting passageways of the sisters' retreat. I kept alert for any signs of Siv. It could be easy to be lulled into a sense of false security with these spellbound owls. Yes, their gizzards were deadened and they appeared to be in a daze, but they were entirely controlled by hagsfiends and capable of rendering great harm. I needed to know if Siv was here, and I needed to see the Glauxess because it was my guess that it was through the gizzard of the Glauxess that the hagsfiends had gained control.

I soon knew I was right. The Nacht Ga' had been cast not just on this one owl, but the entire lot. I entered a large central space in the network of burrows and immediately noticed the strong scent of crow as a Spotted Owl approached. And there was something else. That unmistakable yellow of her eyes was only thinly veiled. One cannot imagine the intensity of the yellow in the eyes of a hagsfiend in the rage of battle. It is said that if one stares straight into a hagsfiend's eyes, one can go blind. But I have long believed that it is not blindness that occurs but a state similar to that of yeepness. In any case, I was prepared. My ice sliver was tucked under the knobby suface of my third toe, ready to be slipped into the gizzard. I just had to get near enough to the Glauxess to use it.

But then something strange began to happen. It felt as if the air in the burrow was vibrating. I knew immediately what it was. Two powerful forces of magic were grazing up against each other: the nachtmagen of the hagsfiends and my magic, for which there was not yet even a word. Invisible sparks between these two forces began to fly. Suddenly, an overpowering flare burst from the eyes of the Glauxess. The burrow flashed with yellow light. She stepped closer. *She is trying to blind me*, I thought. *I will not flinch. I must let her come closer and closer*. I felt myself going yeep, but I was not flying. How could one go yeep if one was already on the ground? It was my gizzard. Glaux, no! *Not my gizzard*, I thought. Panic welled up in me. I felt myself slipping into some sort of trance. I blinked. This was oddly similar to that strange time in Beyond the Beyond when I was entranced by the ember. I had sworn I would never let that happen again. I had failed to act then.

But now something even stranger happened. In my head, there flashed a vision of Fengo and the ember as I had first seen its reflection in that dear wolf's beautiful green eyes. The glare of yellow in the burrow began to dim. *Now!* I thought. *Now is the time!* And I lunged toward the Glauxess with my ice sliver and plunged it deep. And then the yellow receded, the world darkened, and I fell unconscious.

CHAPTER TEN

My Best Intentions

Was I dead or was I dreaming? I seemed to be flying outside my body, high in the winter sky. Where? I was not sure. I do remember seeing the moon suddenly obliterated by what at first I thought were bats in flight. But their wings were too big, and their feathers too long and shaggy. They had to be hagsfiends, yet I felt no fear. When I looked down I saw that they were hurling themselves from the Island of Elsemere. And then I woke up. I was in a burrow. The burrow of the Glauxian Sisters on that same island. I looked around. It took a while for my eyes to adjust. They burned as if they had been seared, as sometimes happens to warriors who fight in daylight and encounter ice glare. But this I knew had not been the case with me. I blinked several times and was soon able to make out dark lumps scattered across the floor of the burrow. *My Glaux!* I thought. *The sisters are dead! The hagsfiends have killed them all.* As if proving this, the heavy stench of crow suddenly assaulted me and here and there a black bit of feather floated down from the burrow's ceiling.

But then I heard a stir from the owl closest to me. It was the Glauxess. She raised her head, then dropped it again with a small gasp. I saw the glint of the ice sliver. Cautiously, I approached her. "Rorkna?" I whispered gently.

"Yes, I answer to that name. What has happened to me? What has happened?" She raised her head again. Then, looking around her, she gasped. "Oh, my dear sisters!" She gave an agonizing cry.

"Don't worry, don't worry. They are not dead," I assured her. "If you are not dead, they are not."

"I have the most awful pain deep in my gizzard."

"I can help you," I said. I hoped I could. I knew I would have to try to remove the ice sliver or else her shattered gizzard would never heal properly.

"Here," I said, grabbing a small rock. "Put this in your beak and bite down hard while I remove this ice sliver."

"An ice sliver!" She gasped. "Why am I not dead?"

"I'll explain later. Just bite down now."

She did, and quickly I nipped at the tip of the ice sliver that protruded from her gizzard through her flesh. She gave a yelp of great pain and swooned. But as she did so, I heard the first rustling of the other owls. The Nacht Ga' had been broken for all of them. They were rousing themselves now, one by one, shaking their heads as if they had been in a long, deep sleep. As the Glauxess was restored, so were they. She had been the key upon which the Nacht Ga' turned.

"How many moons have we been gone?" asked one.

"Gone?" asked another. "I think we have just been asleep."

At that moment, the Glauxess came out of her swoon. She was as perplexed as the others. "Something strange has happened here," she said.

Now, Dear Owl, I was faced with a difficult decision. I could not explain outright to the sisters what had happened to them. As you might recall, I earlier wrote that the orders of the Glauxian Sisters and Brothers believed that hagsfiends existed due to owlkind's desertion of reason and loss of faith in Glaux, that it was this loss of both reason and faith that had allowed the hagsfiends to enter into our world. If I told them how a spell had been cast upon them by a powerful hagsfiend, it might have destroyed them. They might believe they had wavered and this occurred because of their lack of faith. I decided I could not tell them what had happened. It was evident that they were oblivious to the stench of crow. I was probably aware of it because of my newly enhanced senses. No, it was best to keep my own counsel about this. I simply could not reveal to these selfless sisters of Glaux that they had fallen prey to the powers of the hagsfiends and their magic. So I made up a story about the weather. I told them that when the N'yrthnookah blows, a deep, trancelike sleep can afflict some owls. It was a complete lie, but a lie told with the best intentions.

We talked for a long time. I had things I needed to know. And of course, they had questions, too. It was with great patience I explained who I was and where I had come from.

"So," the Glauxess finally said, "I do believe I remember Siv talking of you that summer she came to visit. The three of you were great companions, is that not so?"

"Yes, indeed, Sister, and that is why I have now come. You have heard that good King H'rath died in battle?"

"Oh, yes, indeed. And I grieved for my dear cousin's loss. Might you know where she has gone?"

"I was about to ask the same of you, madam."

"Me?"

"Yes, did you know that she and H'rath were expecting their first chick?"

"No!" Rorkna gasped, and there was a soft tittering among the other sisters.

"Yes, it is true. I thought she might have sought

refuge here, but she didn't?" I paused. "As far as you can remember?"

"I don't think so. But what with this odd sleep that overtook us" — she looked about — "do you suppose that those berries we stored from last summer could have gone bad on us, Sister Lydfryk? I mean, I know Grank thinks it was the N'yrthnookah, but it could have been the berries."

I tried to steer her gently back to the subject. "But you don't think that Siv could have come here recently with her egg?"

"Oh, no." She twisted her head. "I certainly would have remembered if my cousin had shown up here with an egg." She gave a soft churring sound of laughter. But then a tiny little Elf Owl spoke up.

"You know, I don't remember Queen Siv, but I do seem to have a dim recollection of a gadfeather coming here." She turned to a Barred Owl who stood beside her and who was still a bit bleary-eyed. "Do you, Sister?"

"Now that you mention it, yes. And didn't she sing us a song?" This seemed to cause a ripple of excitement among the sisters.

They began remembering the gadfeather with a lovely voice coming and singing them a song.

"Something about the sky is my hollow," said one.

"Yes, and how they need no perch, no home. Very pretty. Slightly impractical, but a beautiful song," said another.

So Siv had not been here. How had I been so wrong? I turned now to Rorkna. "You knew Siv well, madam. Where would she go if she were all alone and with an egg, the egg of her first chick?"

Rorkna blinked and clamped her beak shut as she thought. "In truth, my dear, I would have thought she would have come to me. But if not here . . . well, I do remember that summer when she came to visit, she told me, and I took it as a great compliment that she would confide in me this way, that she and you and H'rath had discovered a marvelous hideaway in some ice cliffs."

The Ice Cliff Palace! Why, of course! Why had I not thought of it? Sister Rorkna must have noticed the look in my eyes. The elation.

"You know what I am talking about?" she asked.

"Yes, madam!" I exclaimed. "I do indeed!"

"Well, go to her and please tell her if she needs our help we are here for her. These are dangerous times, but I doubt anybody would ever attack our retreat."

"No, never," the others murmured in agreement.

"Oh, no — never," I added for good measure. Although I crossed two of my talons for the lie I had just told — with the best of intentions.

CHAPTER ELEVEN
The Ice Cliff Palace

The blizzard had subsided and been followed by sheets of freezing rain. It was a brutal gale-lashed night when I left the Island of Elsemere. Where the sea was free of ice, the water roiled violently, and as I approached the Ice Talons, great blocks of frozen seawater ground against each other, groaning horribly beneath the rage of the wind. The Ice Cliff Palace was on the southwest side of the Talons, far up in a frozen canyon where the cliffs rose eerily into the night. Warped and scraped by thousands upon thousands of years of weather, these cliffs had been carved into bridges and arches and spires. Behind them was a complex maze of interlocking ice passageways. To find one's way to the Ice Cliff Palace in the heart of the cliffs was almost impossible. This made it a perfect hideaway, an unassailable stronghold in desperate times. And these were desperate times. H'rath, Siv, and I had discovered this retreat many years before. Only a few of the king's and queen's most trusted servants knew its whereabouts and even they often became lost in the maze of ice. Rumors had abounded for years as to its location, but despite their powerful magic the hagsfiends had not been able to find it.

Now as I flew up the ice canyon, I scanned the face of the cliffs for a ribbon of darkness that would appear blacker than the night. I knew I would see it soon, but at that same moment I began to smell a vile crowish odor. The hagsfiends were near! I knew at once that I must cease my flight. I could not risk revealing an entryway into the Ice Cliff Palace. I knew I must spottilate immediately so that I could blend in with the ice-sheathed cliffs. This is precisely what I did, and not a moment too soon.

I lighted and stood as tall and thin as possible. It was an intentional wilf in which I pressed my feathers close to my bones. Just then, the noxious odor of hagsfiends swirled around me until I thought I might yarp a pellet. This indeed would be a giveaway, literally a dead give-away! But I swallowed, feeling my first stomach lurch and my gizzard quake as I heard the air hiss with that unmistakable stropping sound. First, I saw the spikes of stiff feathers like daggers rising from a hagsfiend's spine and then a very long tail. *Can it really be Penryck?* It was. The air stirred about me as he flew by so close I could have reached out and touched him. So close that I saw the little half-hags swirling in the currents of his tail feathers. These minute parasitic demon creatures are much smaller and not as strong as hagsfiends, but it is as if all evil has been concentrated in them, distilled to the highest potency. Their beaks are said to drip a kind of poison that hagsfiends themselves are immune to. It is a poison that kills the mites that live in hagsfiends' feathers. The half-hags feed on these mites and are therefore dependent on the hagsfiends for their sustenance. I had pressed my feathers as close to my body as possible and drawn myself up tall, spottilating so as to turn my plummage inside out. In my stillness, my slenderness, and my near whiteness, I was, for all intents and purposes, an icicle — one of many. It seemed to take Penryck forever to fly by. I saw more of his feathers close up than I cared to and more of the half-hag demons. Thankfully, they did not see me. The half-hags have woeful eyesight. Some say it is because they are part bat.

It should be noted here that the plumage of a hagsfiend and a half-hag is as different from that of any true owl as a snakeskin is different from a bear's hide. Hagsfiends' feathers are a deep glistening black, but instead of plummels, those fine fringe feathers that help owls fly so silently, the leading edges of their flight feathers are very long and shaggy and trail through the air, disturbing currents and making a hissing sound. And then, of course, there is the awful stench. There is nothing subtle about a hagsfiend and in many ways this is good. One knows when they are coming. But there are other characteristics of these birds that are truly terrifying. Perhaps they do not need to be subtle. Their beaks are as sharp as any ice blade. Their talons are like ice needles. Indeed, all the weapons we have learned to make from the strong ice — ice needles, ice swords, ice splinters, spiked fizgigs — were invented to combat the deadly sharpness of hagsfiends' beaks and talons.

Penryck finally did pass by, and it was then safe for me to go into the small fracture in the ice cliffs. I threaded my way through the twisting passages. There was a full moon and, as the storm clouds scudded across the sky, an occasional shaft of moonlight fell through the issen clarren, or clear ice, illuminating the interior of this strange, tangled web of ice and frost. There was nothing more beautiful than the Ice Palace in falling shafts of moonlight. Every ice crystal, every flake of snow radiated intricate faceted designs that sparkled fiercely. It was as if the stars had fallen from the sky and hung suspended within these cliffs.

Deep in a maze of ice tunnels and channels I came upon her. There she sat, the widow queen, trembling on the nest of her egg. Her breast was nearly bare from the feathers she had plucked to weave into the packed snow from which she had fashioned her schneddenfyrr, that special kind of nest that we birds of the near-treeless north build for our eggs. These nests are surprisingly snug and warm, and Siv herself was not shivering from cold but from fear. I could see the grief deep in her amber eyes. The stranger at the grog tree had told me about that last battle in which H'rath had been cut down. The queen had witnessed it from an ice notch in the Hrath'ghar palace and had seen the king, her mate, fall in flight, his blood splattering the glacier below. The stranger had said that if she had been in flight instead of sitting on her egg, she would have gone yeep. "As it was, she could hardly move, sir. It seemed as if her gizzard had frozen." When he told me this, I had shut my eyes and imagined her looking into that night that was woven with her mate's blood and seeing the sky torn with hagsfiends. Glaux, how had these creatures ever come to be? What ghastly trick of fate had sent them flying into the owl world with their terrible magic, poisonous enchantments, and vile charms?

But now Siv was there in front of me. My queen, my dear friend, my secret love.

"Grank! Thank Glaux you are here!" She rose from the nest and came to give me a welcome preening, running her beak through my flight feathers. It felt good after the long flight.

"Yes, I am here, Siv." I nodded deeply to her, then turned and greeted her faithful servant, Myrrthe.

"Do you know, I think there was a hagsfiend in the ice canyon tonight?" Siv said. "Both Myrrthe and I caught a strong whiff."

I had not planned to tell her about Penryck, the hagsfiend whom I had just seen. "Don't worry. It's gone now," I said.

"You saw it? Was it male or female?" She blinked rapidly.

"Male. It was Penryck."

"Penryck," she repeated. She seemed relieved and shut her eyes for several seconds. "I was so fearful it might be the one called Ygryk. She is a terrible hagsfiend."

"Yes, I have heard, but not, I think, as bad as Penryck."

"Worse," she said firmly.

"Why is that?"

"She craves this egg of mine, Grank. She is the mate of Pleek now. They cannot have a chick. She's a hagsfiend and he's a Great Horned, so it is impossible. But she wants my egg for her own, for their own. She wants to practice her evil magic on it and transform it into a monster. She wants to be its mother!" Poor Siv nearly gagged on the word "mother." "I am frightened, Grank. There is nothing more terrifying than a hagsfiend who craves a chick."

"There you are wrong, my dear," I replied.

"What do you mean?" Siv asked, genuinely perplexed.

"I mean that there is something more fierce, more violent."

"What is that?"

"A mother whose chick is threatened." I saw a startled look pass through the amber luster of Siv's eyes. "Now step aside, my dear, and let me see the egg."

I came up to the schneddenfyrr. There, nestled in the delicately woven pieces of ice and packed snow, was an egg, an egg the likes of which I had never seen. It was indeed a special egg, so luminous that one might have thought that within its white shell a tiny silvery moon lay cradled. I knew immediately that it was a male. And it came to me that this small male chick who would hatch soon should be called Hoole. Hoole, like the fabled mage of times past, who was thought to be merely an invention to soothe the ruffled spirits and tremulous gizzards of desperate owls in a world overrun by hagsfiends. A Hoole, whose spirit had led the dire wolves to the Beyond!

I looked up now at Siv and our eyes met. A sliver of moonlight came through the issen clarren and ignited tiny amber fires in her eyes. I could read these flames perfectly. A bird in flight, an egg cradled in its talons as it flew across the Bitter Sea. She almost guessed what I was seeing. Her voice trembled as she spoke.

"The egg *is* special, isn't it?" She paused for a long time. I knew that she was thinking of the inevitable choice she must make. I could not tell her. It was not my place. How could I, a male owl, know what it was like to lay an egg — any egg — whether it was luminous like this one or an ordinary white egg?

Finally, Siv spoke: "In order to save him, I must part with him." It was not a question but a statement.

I nodded. "It will simply be too dangerous for you and the egg, Siv. You have every hagsfiend on your tail. They are looking for a queen with an egg. And they will find you. Lord Arrin would love to take your egg. It would give him incredible power if this chick were hatched in his realm, under his stewardship."

"Imagine" — she lowered her voice to barely a whisper as she looked down on the egg, her own face now basking in the luminous light it gave off — "imagine using this precious egg as a thing for evil."

"It is unimaginable."

Siv gave a little shake of her shoulder feathers and straightened herself. She blinked and looked directly at me. "You will take the egg and care for it and raise the chick, then?"

"With all the care and love that I can give. I promise you this, Siv. And if there is a night when you can come to see him . . ." She startled when I said "him," and I nodded and went on, "Siv, if there is a time when the wars are finished and there are no more hagsfiends, I promise I shall send for you."

"Yes, of course, I know you will." Her eyes had begun to stream with tears. She looked down at the egg, and it almost seemed that it was composed entirely of light. It was incandescent and appeared to have no substance save for the unearthly glow that emanated from it. And if the egg was nothing but light, Siv herself had become pure grief.

"Where will you take it, Grank?" she asked.

I breathed a sigh of relief. She had not sensed where I would take this egg.

"I can't tell you, Siv. If I told you, it would endanger not just the egg, but you as well."

"I don't matter," she said quietly.

"Siv, don't say that. You do matter."

"I feel as if I am nothing without my egg, without my mate."

"Now, now, milady." Myrrthe tried to console her mistress, putting a snow-white wing lightly on her shoulder.

"Siv," I said. "You are still a mother, no matter where your chick is. You brought this egg into the world. You shall always be a mother, just as you shall always be a queen."

She looked up around her and murmured, "A queen imprisoned in her own Ice Palace."

At just that moment, there was a loathsome stench. We all froze and then, suddenly, the ice was washed in an eerie yellow glow.

"Hagsfiends!" Siv whispered. "Hagsfiends!"

"Noooo!" A shuddering cry came from Myrrthe, but I turned and saw her swell to twice her size. It was as if a large cumulus cloud had descended into the Ice Cliff Palace.

CHAPTER TWELVE
To the Bitter Sea

At the moment the word "hagsfiend" was uttered, Siv's eyes went through an incredible transformation. The amber beam hardened, as hard as the metals that Fengo and I had extracted from rocks, as hard as the strong ice from which we made our swords. She grabbed an ice scimitar that had been H'rath's and rushed out into the tunnel, ordering Myrrthe to go in an opposite direction. "You know where we'll meet, Myrrthe." It was not a question.

"Yes, milady," Myrrthe replied, and picked up a small ice dagger for herself.

I knew immediately what Siv planned. She was going to decoy them, distract them. I reached for the egg and, clutching it with my talons, made for a back passageway out of the Ice Cliff Palace. I had no idea if I would ever see Siv again. But only moments before I had said that a mother whose chick was threatened was fiercer and more violent than any hagsfiend. The time to prove this had come.

Once I had left the Ice Cliff Palace, I headed across the Bay of Fangs on a straight course for the Bitter Sea. There was an island there with a dense forest and trees with good hollows where I thought the egg and I would be safe. In general, owls of the N'yrthghar nest in ground burrows or the ice caves of a glacier or the many cliffs of ice along the coastline. We do not like tree nests. We prefer the solidness of ice and find the dank hollows and swaying of the trees in the wind uncomfortable. So I knew that this isolated place would be good for minding the egg until it hatched. There was also another reason I wanted to go to the forest: I had brought with me from the Beyond an interesting object that Fengo and I had made out of the metal we had drawn from rock. We had experimented with it, heating it up and then bending it. We had succeeded in shaping it into a small container of sorts, no bigger really than a very large acorn or perhaps a tiny owl's egg. And in that container — a cupper we called it — I had brought, in addition to the coals that were tucked into the moose horn, a bonk coal swaddled in a special moss that grew in the Beyond. The moss kept the coal glowing and hot and yet the coal did not melt the metal. The bonk coal, along with the ones in the moose horn, were the first ever brought to the N'yrthghar. And I planned to make great use of them. Not only for experiments with metals, but for flame reading. If I must stay on that remote island in a forest, thick with trees, tending this egg and the young chick that would hatch from it, it was essential for me to know what was happening in the rest of the kingdom. The trick would be to ignite a small fire without burning down the rest of the forest.

That wintry night, I found a place on the island where the trees grew tall and straight. Between the highest branches of an ice-sheathed tree, there were two hollows. One was the perfect size for an orphan egg and its foster father, and the larger one a perfect size for a collier and his fire. I knew I could line one hollow with soft moss, tucked in tightly around the egg, along with twigs and fir needles and scraps from the forest, besides the more traditional materials of snow and ice. It would be perfect for a nest. The other hollow — the fire hollow — I would pack only with snow and make a small pit for my coal. Then I would gather strips of birch bark for what I came to call the Telling Fire.

I was desperate to know how Siv had fared, and as soon as I tucked the egg in I went to the other hollow and began to pack it with snow. I decided to use the bonk coal. So from my coal cupper, I withdrew the glowing ember. As the flames ignited I leaned forward. What would I see?

At first, the images were pale and quivering. It was hard to make out any shapes at all, let alone owls. I thought I spied a ragged black smear that could have been a hagsfiend. Then I soon realized that there was more than one. They were definitely hagsfiends. How would Siv and Myrrthe survive this? Things became more distinct. I saw a glimmer, like the mist that rises at twilight in this land of the North Waters, and arced above it was a silver curving radiance — the ice scimitar of H'rath raised to attack.

CHAPTER THIRTEEN
Blood Snowflakes

Siv flew with a lumpish ball of snow and ice in her talons and an ice scimitar in her beak. I could tell that the stench of hagsfiends was almost overpowering her. She staggered in flight but only briefly. The two hagsfiends were coming toward her at great speed. If they pinned her against the ice wall, she would be finished. But she had one thing in her favor: They still believed that she had the egg. With the ball of snow and ice clutched in her talons, she led them on a chase. As long as they believed that this ball was the egg, they would be careful because they wanted to snatch it from her. But now they were backing her toward an ice wall and very soon they would discover that it was not an egg that she clutched in her talons. Suddenly, the night flinched and the blackness throbbed with a glaring yellow light. The moon, the stars turned yellow. The snow "egg" began to slip from her talons. Her wings were beginning to fold. Her gizzard grew still. But she was not going yeep. It was far worse.

The hypnotic yellow glare of the hagsfiends' eyes had bathed the entire world around her. It was at this moment of the yellow glare's greatest intensity that Siv spread her wings, dropped the ice ball, took the ice scimitar in her talons, and rushed with an unmatched speed straight for the hagsfiends.

The harsh yellow light began to recede. The white swirling madness of the blizzard returned and in the flames of my fire I watched in horror as the snowflakes turned red with blood. I felt my gizzard tremble as I saw an entire upper wing torn off in flight. I leaned closer to the fire. Was that wing black? Was it brown with spots? There was too much blood to tell, and then the images began to dissolve. They simply melted away. I blinked once, twice. I was often exhausted after seeking visions in the flames of a fire, but I had never before felt so weakened. I knew that I must return to the other hollow. My duty was to the egg, guarding it and nurturing the chick who would break from it. I must put Siv out of my mind. It tore at my gizzard to think of her dead, murdered by those hagsfiends, but it was the life within the egg that counted now. Siv trusted me. Whether she was dead or alive, that trust must never be broken. But I knew that those feathers drenched in blood would haunt my dreams for the rest of my life. My one great love, Siv of the Hrath'ghar, was gone.

It would be a long time before I dared build another Telling Fire. My concentration had to be on the egg. And it was. I plucked down from my breast feathers every day. I burrowed in the snow for old leaves that had dropped from the trees, then dried them and tucked them into the nest. I poked at rotting logs to find where the plumpest grubs might be for the chick's first food after it had hatched.

The forest itself had a different kind of silence from the rest of the N'yrthghar. There was not the groan of grinding ice, but the trees creaked in the wind. There were many land creatures but none of air. And that was fine with me. It was a strangely peaceful place, and I felt far away from the wars and the hagsfiends, away from the chaos and the blood — except the blood that haunted my dreams, the blood of Siv. But I had sworn not to build a fire and look into those telling flames, at least until the chick had hatched.

Of course, I could not resist. I made another fire. But again I made the mistake of hunting for visions rather than letting them come to me. The odd thing was that I did see something in those flames that possibly could have been coming toward this lonely tree-clad island in the Bitter Sea, but I paid it no heed. It appeared to me as a small smudge in the most unstable region of the flame. You must understand that when I was in the Beyond, and Fengo and I were experimenting with fire, we isolated four distinct regions within a flame. Fengo, of course, could not read the flames as I could and he was only interested in them for their utilitarian value — how we could coax metal from rock, or change sand into glossen. But I found that the clearest images always came to me from what we called the pale fire region, which is usually at the vortex of the flame.

I knew it was useless searching the flames for Siv. Her image would appear when it did. But at least building this fire revived my interest in my previous study of flames and the various effects of fire on different materials. I especially wanted to explore the possibilities of using fire and ice in some combination to improve our weapons. Could, for example, the edge of an ice scimitar made with issen blaue be honed to a new sharpness by exposing it to that peculiar region in the flame that Fengo and I called the "yellow curved plane"?

These activities would help pass the time until the

hatching of the chick. The egg did not have to be sat upon constantly. I had found enough moss in this beautiful forest to tuck in and around the schneddenfyrr and make it all warm and cozy. And this brings me to a point that I have never thought of before: Caring for an egg was no easy task. When my siblings were eggs and then hatchlings, my parents spelled each other in the nest. One would hunt while the other sat on the egg or tended the new chicks. Sitting on an egg constantly is about as boring as watching ice melt. And then, of course, after it hatches, nothing is boring. Those little beaks always wide open, begging for food, squeaking away, whining, crying. At least I would only have one to tend and, prince or not, I knew he would be squawking and demanding, making a mess in the nest, and if he was like any other hatchling, trying to fly before his wings were fully fledged. Sometimes I grew weak at the very thought of parenthood and all I had taken on.

Despite this, I knew that within this egg that glowed with remarkable light was a chick who would grow into an owl like no other. And this forest with its trees wrapped in ice was the perfect refuge for us. Yes, I had begun to think of this egg and myself as "us." Destiny had bound us together as strongly as if I were this chick's father. But more than father or mother, I would become this hatchling's tutor and if what I had come to suspect was true, the destiny of the entire owl kingdom would rest upon him. I knew that the ember was somehow part of his special destiny. I had been too weak to deal with the owl ember myself. I simply did not have the Ga'. But I sensed that this unborn chick did have it. It was the Ga' of this chick that made the egg so luminous. Now my fears of managing a demanding chick paled in comparison to the responsibilities this young owl would have to bear. A boy king would soon hatch. I sensed it would happen when the night was the longest and the day the shortest, and for that I must wait patiently and be constantly alert.

Although I was never was far from the tree, I had begun to build fires outside of the fire hollow, in between the boulders that were strewn about in the forest. Each day I was discovering new things. In the Beyond, the land was scattered with nuggets of copper, gold, and silver. Here I found no such rocks, and I could not go as far to look for materials as Fengo had. I had to make do with what was near. But I did find red rocks that I sensed might contain metal. The bonk coal I had brought with me had, of course, hatched other coals, but no bonk ones. Those could be caught only on the fly, spit from an intense fire. There is no such thing as a second-generation bonk coal. This was a problem, for I knew that these rocks from which I hoped to draw metal were very tough and needed a very hot fire.

So I experimented with ways to increase the heat by other means. And it was through these trials that I invented a special fireplace that I came to call a "forge." Near the tree where my hollow was located, there was one immense boulder that, through some cataclysmic event in our earth's history, had a large crack that nearly split it in two. I had been studying this crack for some time. The ground breezes of the forest seemed to funnel directly into it, and then pass out the top of the crack. I began to think that this might provide the drafts that are so critical to the feeding of fires. So I started building fires inside the cracked boulder.

It was hot, dirty work. My snowy-white spots turned sooty. My talons grew black. Although my original intent had been to coax metal from the hard red rock, I instead experimented with what kind of fires I could build in the split of this boulder. By this time, I was so absorbed with the different kinds of fires I could construct and the varying intensity of the heat that I rarely looked deeply into the flames to read them. Had I studied those flames I would not have seen Siv, but that smudge in the sky I had first noticed some days before. But I did not. It was only when I began to sense someone watching me that I grew uneasy and tried again to read the flames. I was shocked when I saw the image of a youthful Great Horned Owl flickering in the curve of the flame. Indeed, he was, at that very moment, roosting in the large blue spruce behind me! I spun my head around and blinked in astonishment. There he was — perched on a high branch — watching me. My gizzard seized.

CHAPTER FOURTEEN
The Arrival of Theo

"I want to learn."

Those were Theo's first words to me.

But how much had he seen already? I wondered. And does he know about the egg? How could I have been such a fool to ignore that smudge at the edge of the flames? How could I have thought I was so entirely alone, so isolated here when this owl was practically within yarping distance of me? And how long had he been here on the island?

"W-w-w . . . what do you want to learn?" I stammered.

"About fire." He flew down from the tree and landed on the boulder.

I fluffed my feathers in a dismissive way. "You're too young. It takes patience, maturity, and I'm sure you don't have the temperament."

"How can you tell? You only just met me. You don't even know my name, let alone my temperament."

What gallgrot, I thought. "You're a Great Horned," I replied.

"What does that have to do with it?"

"They're impulsive."

"That's unfair. You can't just exclude someone because of his breed. Besides, it's untrue. I can't help being young. I can't help being a Great Horned. But I am mature, and I am not impulsive." He paused as if waiting for me to reply. But I turned my back on him and peered into the fire, trying not to read the flames. But his face was everywhere in those flames.

"Don't you want to know my name?" he asked.

"No," I muttered.

"My name is Theo, and do you know what you are?" He did not wait for an answer. "You're rude."

I had a feeling that I was not going to get rid of this young'un that fast. "So what do you want to learn, and why do you think you can?"

"I want to learn the art of fire and of smeisshen."

"Smeisshen?"

"Smeisshen — you know, striking, hitting hard ice."

The word was, I wagered, from a very old form of Krakish, the kind they spoke way up in one of the firths. They loved the old language in those firths. They kept words, polishing them as if they were precious stones.

"Where are you from, young'un?"

"Firth of Grundenspyrr, off the Firth of Fangs."

"Thought so," I replied.

"So now you are going to tell me that owls from a far firth won't have the brains for this."

"I didn't say that. But I might point out that it is not ice I have been smeisshening, as you say, but rock."

"It's *schmeiss huch ning* — that is how you pronounce it. Cough a little where the word breaks and you'll have it."

"Oh, so now you are a language expert."

"I never said such a thing. I just know how to speak old Krakish, that's all."

"Pretty full of yourself, aren't you?" As you can see, I could be fairly obnoxious.

"I'm not full of myself. If I were I wouldn't be here asking you to teach me. I would think I knew everything."

This took me aback. I blinked at him.

"You know," he said, stepping closer, "I had an uncle once. He died in the Siege of the Fangs — murdered by hagsfiends. He was a great teacher. He believed that knowledge was a sacred trust. He believed that knowledge, not necessarily knowledge of magic but knowledge of the natural world, was the one way we could overcome the hagsfiends." He paused. I didn't say anything. This was an interesting young owl. There was no doubt about it. "My uncle said, 'I teach because I was taught.'"

I felt a quiver in my gizzard. "But nobody taught me this," I replied, gesturing at the fire. I knew that sounded rather lame. The youngster agreed.

"I expected a better answer from you," Theo replied. There was not a trace of smugness in his voice. There was only disappointment. He looked at me through his aggrieved tawny yellow eyes. It was this expression that broke me.

I sighed. "All right. I'll take you on as an apprentice. But we're going to have a few rules."

"Oh, yes! Yes! I'll do anything you say, sir! Anything." He lofted himself straight up and down at least three times, such was his excitement. "Anything. I'm very obedient."

"I'll bet," I muttered. "So, these are the rules. While you are here learning from me, it is strictly forbidden to leave the island."

He nodded.

"Furthermore, your business is to learn about fire, nothing else. Understand?"

"Well, what would you define as 'else'?"

I gaped and blinked at him in amazement. The impudence! The sheer gallgrot!

"I mean you keep your beak out of anything that is not connected with fire."

"Like the egg?"

Now I was truly stunned. "The egg? You know about the egg?"

He looked down at his talons and scratched them nervously on the boulder. "Well, yes. I figured that was why you were digging down for the snow moss. It's always used in schneddenfyrrs."

I was tempted to ask him how long he had been here but frankly did not want to give him the satisfaction of saying, "Oh, ten or twelve nights," thus proving that I was too stupid to have noticed. I coughed slightly. "Err . . . yes. I am sitting for friends of mine who are unable to care for the egg because of the war. They are off fighting."

"Oh, that reminds me," Theo said suddenly.

"Reminds you of what?"

"I don't fight." I blinked at him. "I am a gizzard resister. I don't believe in war. In my gizzard, I believe there is always a better way. And I don't believe in magic, either."

"Are you a Glauxian Brother?"

"I would like to be. But they think I am not quite ready."

"And you didn't make them take you anyway?" *How come I got stuck with you?* I wanted to scream.

"In matters of faith, one cannot use force. It's difficult to explain," he said.

"I can't believe it!"

"Believe what?" Theo asked.

"That it's difficult to explain. You never seem to be at a loss for words, Theo."

"Could we get on with the rules?" he pressed.

"That's about it. I keep a clean camp. Find your own hollow."

"Thank you . . . thank you so much, sir. I'll be the best student you've ever had."

"I've never had a student!"

"Well, I'm sure we'll both learn a lot, then. I, as a student, and you, as a teacher. And if you need any help in tending the egg, don't hesitate to ask."

I glared at him now. "No! The egg is my business. Learning about the fire and the forge is yours."

"Yes, sir! Yes, sir. I promise to be an attentive, hard-working apprentice. I want to learn."

And learn he did. The irony of all this was that as I had become the first collier, Theo the gizzard resister would become the first blacksmith and learn how to shape black metal into incomparable weapons — weapons as deadly as ice swords, ice slivers, or ice scimitars. I quickly altered that old Krakish word "smeisshen" to something I could pronounce without gagging. The word became "smith" — and then blacksmith, for we were soon able to extract a new kind of metal that was much harder than any I had encountered in the Beyond, and it turned black when it cooled.

CHAPTER FIFTEEN

A Wounded Queen

My last vision of Siv in the flames had been a terrible one indeed. I had seen her caught in that horrifying searing yellow light that radiated from the hagsfiends' eyes, then taking the scimitar and rushing at the hagsfiends, and the sudden terrible sight of a torn wing and blood, lots and lots of blood. Since that time I had been too frightened to scour the flames for any other sight of Siv. I had sensed that she had survived. She would later tell me that just before she charged the hagsfiends, she feared that she was turning into one.

"So this is nachtmagen!"

That was her last thought before she felt her mind scraped clean. And then no thoughts, no feelings. It was as if she were becoming nothing. Or was she becoming something else? Something pecked at her gizzard. There was a peculiar ringing at the back of her mind. "Am I becoming a hagsfiend?" She felt her plummels dissolve in the cold night air. And where they had been, she felt the edges become ragged. She looked in horror as her beautiful white-spotted, rich brown feathers began to darken. "No!" she shrieked.

But she was not becoming a hagsfiend. No, my friend, it was the Nacht Ga'. The dreadful spell had been cast, and Siv was resisting it with all of her might. Only to herself did her plumage appear to change. Outwardly, to anyone else, she would seem the same. What was changing was her gizzard and within it the seeds of her Ga'. It was at that moment when she dimly perceived these strange gizzardly mutations that she cried out with a bellow worthy of the mightiest warrior, "No!" and charged the hagsfiends. It was at that moment that I lost her image in the flames, when the harsh yellow light receded and the snowflakes turned red.

It was much later still that I would learn that all the while I was tending the egg, Siv was not dead but grievously wounded, her port wing nearly torn off. She had been able to fly only with Myrrthe's help in a kronkenbot, a windless kind of vacuum used for transporting wounded soldiers from a battle. Normally, it would have taken a minimum of two owls to create the kronkenbot, but Myrrthe was determined, and if there was anything Snowy Owls of the far north were known for, it was their unfaltering resolve, their sheer stubbornness.

"I can do it, milady, I can do it. The tailwind is favorable. I know I can do it." By ruddering her lateral tail feathers and making minuscule adjustments to her primaries, Myrrthe was somehow creating a windless space in which Siv, still bleeding, could be sucked along in flight. It was this sudden favorable wind change that had initially allowed them to escape because the wind brought with it the risk of salt death for the hagsfiends. You see, Dear Owl, despite all their powers, hagsfiends feared one thing: salt water from our icy seas. They could be seriously wounded or even killed by seawater. Their drenched feathers lacked oil and could not shed the salty water. Thus, their wings iced up immediately, often causing them to plummet into the sea. They avoided any contact with seawater.

It was for this reason that both Siv and Myrrthe knew that they would be safest in one of the sea-washed caves of an upper firth where a warm current helped keep the water fairly free of ice. Myrrthe had been scouring the coast for just this sort of refuge as they flew well up into the Firth of Fangs.

"Anything yet?" Siv gasped.

"Nothing so far, milady." Myrrthe angled her wings and turned into a narrow inlet, which she believed was called the Firthkin of N'or, and which pierced far into the Hrath'ghar glacier. It was a narrow, deep channel. It rarely froze except in the very coldest weather, and yet, because of the odd currents, icebergs occasionally floated through it.

"Milady!" Myrrthe suddenly said. "Would you consider sheltering on an iceberg?"

"My dear Myrrthe." Siv's voice had become low and guttural. The words tore from her beak, jagged and nearly incomprehensible. But despite her pain, she managed to maintain a sense of humor. "At this moment, I would consider anything, even a seagull's nest!"

Myrrthe blinked in astonishment. The notion of this regal queen occupying the same quarters as a wet pooper was beyond the bizarre.

"That shan't be necessary, milady."

Myrrthe peered down and briefly studied the iceberg they were flying over. There were overhanging beaks of ice undercut with shelves that might offer up caves. At this point, however, there was little choice. Myrrthe knew that she had to get Siv to a roosting spot quickly. And her own wings ached. Her refined feather adjustments were becoming sloppier by the second. It was imperative that they find something now.

"All right," she announced. "We're going down. Stay in position, milady. Don't move."

"I doubt that I'm going anywhere, Myrrthe."

The berg was an amazing creation. It was, as Siv would

later say, "the berg of all bergs," so intricately carved by sea and wind and currents, it was a veritable labyrinth of ice and water. A perfect refuge.

"This is it!" Siv gasped as they landed. "I know it in my gizzard. I know it in my plummels, or what's left of them!"

It did not take Myrrthe long to find the perfect cavern. Washed by the jade-green waters of the firthkin, it offered an ideal defense against the hagsfiends. Here, Siv knew she could wait and heal. *But wait for what?* she wondered. The hatching of a chick she might never see, in a distant place she knew not where, in a schneddenfyrr that she had not made? She told herself that she must not dwell on such matters. Healing was her first task. If she could not heal, she was useless to her chick — if, indeed, she should ever meet the hatchling — and useless to her kingdom.

Her port wing was a wreckage of fractured shafts and feathers. The flight feathers on it were gone, the secondaries almost demolished.

Myrrthe immediately sprang into action. She had to stop that bleeding. So taking talonsful of snow and ice, she packed Siv's wound.

"That feels good," Siv said. "But do you think I'll ever fly again?"

"Of course, milady. Just think of this as a violent molt."

If Siv hadn't been in such excruciating pain, she might have laughed. "More snow, Myrrthe. It numbs the pain."

"Yes, dear, I know. And ice will even be better."

The ice did begin to relieve the agony. The bleeding stopped. "Do you remember your first molt, Myrrthe?" Siv asked.

"My first molt. Oh, my goodness, milady. I am so old. How could I ever remember back that far?"

"But it must be interesting for a Snowy because you might not even notice it, what with all your white feathers and all the snow and ice of the N'yrthghar." Siv's voice was growing thick.

"You forget, madam, that when we are hatchlings, we are not yet pure white. We're rather sooty in appearance, if anything."

"I remember my first real molt." Siv's speech was slow and dreamy. "I don't count the ones when my down fell off. I was barely old enough to remember. But the first real one — Great Glaux, I was so shocked. Here, I had just fledged and really mastered flight. I felt so grown up after months of being a hatchling with all that patchy fluff. I had just begun to enjoy my plummels, primaries, secondaries, and my lovely lulus, when all of a sudden, there was a gorgeous tawny brown feather on the ground." Siv's speech slurred a bit.

"Time to rest, dear. You must rest."

"Yes . . . I must rest."

"Remember your great-aunt Agatha. She got better, didn't she?"

"Yes, Aunt Agatha, of course."

Siv hadn't thought of her aunt Agatha in years, but her great-aunt had been terribly wounded in a catastrophic encounter with hagsfiends long ago in the Bitter Sea. During this battle, not one but both of her wings had been horribly maimed. She had been a superb warrior, but she never could fly the position of first ice sliver again. Nonetheless, she had recovered enough to fly in combat. This time as strategic commander of the Ice Scimitar Brigade. She had developed a superb talon technique with the reverse ice scimitar, a very oddly shaped weapon that was perfectly suited for her peculiar wing configurations. Aunt Agatha's amazing courage and determination had been the source of that most famous Krakish motto: "Cintura Vrulcrum, Niykah Kronig," which roughly translates to "Every wound a new opportunity, every curse a new challenge."

Siv drifted off to sleep with one thought. *I must heal. I must heal. I must heal. So much to be done.*

"I need fish!" Siv said when she awoke. Myrrthe greeted this news with mixed emotions. She was overjoyed that her dear lady was hungry. This was a good sign. But at the same time she felt her gizzard crinkle. *She needs fish!* Myrrthe thought. *What she needs is a Fish Owl!*

"Yes, milady, fish oil is the best remedy for rebuilding splintered feather shafts."

"Can you get on with it?" Siv pressed. But she immediately felt guilty for being so peremptory with her dear servant. Although her port wing sent ripples of pain through her body, she knew that this was no cause for rudeness. "I'm sorry. So sorry, Myrrthe. How insensitive of me. I know no more about catching fish than you do. Forgive my rudeness."

"No need, milady. Just let me think a moment."

"Take all the time you need, Myrrthe."

CHAPTER SIXTEEN

A Polar Bear Named Svenka

In her day, Myrrthe had seen a few Fish Owls, and now she tried to remember how they performed the complex feat of plunging through the water's surface and coming back up with a nice fat fish. She was fairly sure that one had to begin the dive from very high up and come in on a fairly steep angle. She thought about it several more minutes and then perched herself at the edge of the cavern and peered down into the water. She supposed she would have to keep her eyes open under the water. Not a pleasant thought!

"All right, milady. I'll give it a go."

"Good luck, Myrrthe," Siv said.

But Myrrthe was already spiraling upward in flight.

She tried once, twice, then three and four times. She was keeping her eyes open underwater but she never saw anything. She hated the rush of bubbles and the deafening sound of the water roaring by her ear slits.

On her fifth try, a single word rang out in this isolated firthkin:

"WRONG!"

Myrrthe pulled out of the spiraling plunge and lighted on top of the iceberg.

"Who said that?" She looked around and saw nothing but another iceberg floating by. But suddenly, part of the iceberg rose up and a furry, clawed paw poked at the sky. Myrrthe blinked.

"You're starting too high." It was a polar bear. Myrrthe had seen them many times from a distance but never had met, let alone spoken, to one. In the N'yrthghar there was very little exchange or communication among species. The bear swam up to the edge of the berg and, resting both paws, peered up at Myrrthe with its small close-set dark brown eyes. The iceberg tipped, the edge now buried in the water. Myrrthe began to slide and gripped the ice with her talons.

She had never seen such hugeness, such enormity, such byggenbrocken. Every word for "gigantic" flooded through Myrrthe's head, but then she realized with a start that she was not even seeing half of this bear. Its coat was thick and creamy in color and, although the fur was tightly packed, Myrrthe could see very black skin beneath it where the coat creased as the bear's paws spread on the iceberg. Its shoulders and neck had a bunched look, and Myrrthe bet that, if swimming at full speed, this bear could ram an iceberg in half. Its ears, round and stubby, were rather adorable. "Look," the bear said, "when you're finished staring at me I'll give you some tips on fishing."

"Oh, sorry, so sorry. How rude of me!" Myrrthe said.

"You've never seen one of us close up?"

"Not this close."

"Well, your loss," the bear said blithely. Then in a more companionable manner, she said, "Might I offer some suggestions on where you are going wrong in your fishing attempts?"

"Please do."

"It's simple," the bear explained. "You're coming in too steep. Face it, you don't have the power or the bulk to go really deep for the larger fish. You have to stick to the surface ones — the herring, the silver slips, the bluescales." With one large paw, the bear swept the water and deposited a small mound of squirming tiny bluish fish on the iceberg. Myrrthe gasped.

"Bluescales," said the bear, nosing them up higher so they wouldn't slip off. "They're running now. They'll help your queen."

"Great Glaux, you know?"

"Don't worry. Your secret is safe with me. And as you might have noticed, this firthkin is rather desolate, few creatures about. Just me, really."

"And who are you? How do you call yourself?"

"Oh, how quaint! How do you call yourself! I love it. You owls give such a nice twist to Krakish," the bear said in a friendly way. "My name is Svenka. And yours?"

"Myrrthe. I have served the queen from the time before she was queen. I was her nursemaid, then her governess."

"And the king, I understand, has been killed."

"Yes." Myrrthe did not mention anything about the egg. The less said about that, the better. "Have you heard anything of the wars?"

"Very little. King H'rath is dead. Lord Arrin has gained new territory on the Hrath'ghar glacier. They say that his scouts go out and press young owls into his army. But as I said, I hear very little. I spend most of my time alone and away from all that." Svenka waved a paw dismissively as if to say that the owls' world was no concern of hers.

"But why are you here alone?" Myrrthe asked.

"That is the nature of polar bears. We are solitary creatures. We come together during mating season. And then we part. If we are lucky and have cubs, they stay with us until they can go out on their own."

"Do you have cubs?"

"Not yet, but soon." Svenka pushed off from the iceberg and rolled onto her back. She patted her stomach. "Two, possibly three."

"In there?" Myrrthe said.

"We're not birds, my dear. We don't lay eggs. Our young don't hatch. They get born. We give birth."

Myrrthe blinked and cocked her head thoughtfully. "It's a good system. Convenient. No nest building. No guarding the nest. They're just with you all the time. Better than our way, I think. One might almost wish . . ."

"Don't even think of it, Myrrthe. You're a bird. Birds are birds, bears are bears. Glaux, as you call the great spirit, knows what is best for each creature."

"But what do you call your Glaux?"

"Great Ursa, but it is all the same spirit. No matter what you call it."

"But how can that be?"

"Are you sure you want to get into this now? Shouldn't you take these bluescales to your lady?"

"Oh, you're right, of course."

And so Myrrthe did take the fish to Siv, but the conversation would soon continue. It became the first of several philosophical discussions between the polar bear and the Snowy Owl — until the night that Myrrthe vanished.

CHAPTER SEVENTEEN
Vanished!

Siv couldn't tell me about that horrible night without breaking down. "Everything had been going so well, Grank, so well. I was healing. Myrrthe had learned to fish and then one night..." She began to sob. "I begged her not to go. Hunting lemmings on a moon-bleached night in the middle of winter when their coats had turned white. How would she ever see them? But she argued that I needed the meat now to heal completely."

Myrrthe, you see, Dear Owl, had an expert's knowledge of lemmings and kept track of their cycles and movements. She knew their range, and where they built their nests and tunnels in the shallow spaces between the everfrost and the surface of the tundra. Unlike many of the other non-bird creatures who hibernated during the winter, lemmings did not. They were busy foraging, eating constantly, and doing what they really did best — making babies. No animal can reproduce faster than a lemming. Myrrthe often thought how stupid this was, for, in truth, it was their undoing. About once every four years, the nests became overcrowded and, like idiots, the rodents raced to find new homes. No planning whatsoever. They would just up and leave, the entire mob, often hundreds of thousands of them. Not heeding where they were going, many fell off cliffs into the sea. And they seemed to never learn!

Myrrthe was counting on the lemmings' stupidity and her knowledge of the range. She knew that not far in from the firthkin, on the edges of the Hrath'ghar glacier, there was a colony that had started four years earlier and was about to burst from overcrowding. "With seven litters a year and eleven babies a litter, there must be squillions of them, milady," Myrrthe had told Siv. So off she flew one moonlit windless night when the water in the firthkin was so still that nary a ripple wrinkled its surface. Myrrthe knew lemmings in any season. And Siv, who had flown with her on many past expeditions, knew that she would look first for the puckering up of the land into the ridges and depressions created by the seasonal thawings and freezings. These ridges became the travel routes for the migrating lemmings. Myrrthe would fly over these ridges and, as she told Siv, "Bring back a nice juicy little fellow for my queen."

Siv waited.

*　　*　　*

As dawn melted into morning the next day, there was no sign of the faithful old Snowy. But Siv did not begin to worry until that evening at tween time, those seconds between the last drop of the daylight and the first tinge of the lavender twilight. Siv had not long to wait, for these were among the very shortest days and longest nights of the year. As Siv watched the lavender deepen to purple and then the purple turn to black, she felt her gizzard begin to crumble. Something must have happened, for surely Myrrthe would not let her wait this long with no food. And not even Svenka was around. *Oh, Glaux*, Siv thought. *This cannot be happening. My mate has been killed, my egg taken, and now my dearest and most faithful friend is gone.*

Siv knew that Myrrthe was much more than her nurse-maid and servant. With her dear Myrrthe gone, Siv thought she would starve to death not from lack of food but from lack of those she loved. A wing could mend, but could a broken heart and gizzard ever heal?

Two days later, there was still no sign of Myrrthe, and Siv began to seriously doubt that she herself would survive. She could not yet fly. She had no food. But oddly, she felt no hunger — except in her heart, for even Svenka had left. She was trying to imagine where the polar bear had gone when, suddenly, the immense head poked through the water just as the sun was beginning to rise. The moment Siv saw her dark lusterless eyes she knew something terrible had happened.

"Your cubs? You gave birth and they died? You lost them?"

"No." Svenka shook her head. Siv opened her beak but not a sound came out. The words would not form. "She's gone, Siv," Svenka said, her voice breaking.

"You mean — dead?" Siv asked hoarsely. Svenka nodded. "But how can you be sure?" The bear put a huge paw on the berg and ever so gently placed in front of Siv a snowy white feather from the coverts of Myrrthe's wing. Siv blinked. "She's molted. I'm sure. Myrrthe always molts at odd times."

"No, Siv. I found her."

Siv shook her head trying to understand all this. "What do you mean?" She blinked rapidly.

"She was torn apart."

Siv blinked again. The confusion that swam in her eyes vanished. "Hagsfiends! Hagsfiends are the only ones who kill that way." Although Siv had been wilfing seconds before, she now seemed to swell up in the classic threat display known as thronkenspeer. "Tell me. Tell me everything. Spare me nothing. I must honor her death as I did that of my beloved mate. She was no mere servant. She died for me, didn't she?"

"Most likely. I think I arrived shortly after it had happened."

"How did you know to go looking?"

"On the night she left, just before dawn I got a craving — as many expectant polar bear mothers do — for a bit of anchovy. I knew that the best anchovies this time of year swim near the fringe ice of the Hrath'ghar glacier. So I went."

CHAPTER EIGHTEEN
Svenka Tells a Tale of Death

"I was gorging, I admit, on some of the best anchovies that ever swam in the Great North Waters. It disgusts me now when I think of it."

"It shouldn't," Siv interrupted. "You were nourishing your unborn. What could be more noble?"

"Well, as I rolled over in the water to digest and pat my stomach with the babes inside, I was surprised to see a ragged dark patch appear overhead. At first, I thought it was a weather front coming in. But then tattered shadows began to skim across the still waters. Remember how windless it was on the night she left?" Siv nodded. "Well, there was still no wind. And the water was perfectly still and, with the full-shine moon, every shadow was printed on the water. It was an amazing sight. I had a terrible feeling deep in my gut. My babes seemed to roil within me, sensing my own fear. I knew that Myrrthe had gone for lemmings. I had heard you begging her not to go. But she was right, you did need meat."

"No, no." Siv shook her head in despair.

"Well, I decided I had to go a-land. So I climbed out of the firth and followed those shadows. I began to see that unmistakable silky movement across the glacier. It appeared as if the ground was pulsing. It heaved and swelled. It was the lemmings, white as the snow in their winter pelts, surging across the landscape. It is an unforgettable sight.

"And Myrrthe sailed overhead, plunging down at intervals to attack. The sea of lemmings would part, just like water as it meets an obstacle but, then mindlessly, the animals would flow back together. They showed no panic. They seemed barely conscious that one of their own had been taken. It was as if their brains, what little they have, were fixed on one thing — movement. No destination in mind, no thought of their course, just forward. They were no longer individuals, single creatures. They were the surge, and the surge was them. It was easy pickings for Myrrthe.

"But unlike the lemmings, I could see that she was immediately aware of the danger. She veered off sharply to port. Her strategy was to get back to the water, any water at that point."

Once again, Siv shook her head. "If only she had been diving for fish. They wouldn't have followed her to open water."

"Yes, indeed. They were on her so fast. I raced toward her, stomping on only Great Ursa knows how many hundreds of lemmings. I reared up in the night."

It was Siv who told me this, Dear Owl, and it was as if she had witnessed it all herself. "You can't imagine how it must have been, Grank." She described this enormous white bear. "So huge, so immense," she said, "that you felt she could pluck the moon from the sky." Siv continued Svenka's tale exactly as it had been told to her.

"But it was to no avail," Svenka recounted. "For suddenly, a terrible yellow light began filtering into the moon-pale night. I saw strange shapes, like rags, streaking across the full moon. Now you must understand that we polar bears have little experience with hagsfiends. We don't fly, and they don't swim. I knew nothing of their ways. So although I batted at a few of them and I think injured some gravely, when that yellow glare began to envelop me, I felt completely paralyzed. I sank to the ground, crushing dozens of lemmings beneath me. And still they flowed over me, determined not to alter their course. And I, on my back, could see it all."

Siv said she tried to imagine this mountainous furry animal with lemmings crawling all over her. She understood that weird paralysis as the yellow light seeped from the hagsfiends' eyes. "I don't know how I ever escaped it," Siv said. "How I ever broke from it."

But I know, Dear Owl, how she escaped it: Ga'! I doubted that King H'rath had Ga', despite his being a king of infinite goodness and courage. In that moment, however, as Siv told me of her escape when she was up against the ice wall, I knew in my heart and my mind and, most important, in my gizzard, that she had Ga'.

Svenka continued her story: "The worst part about it was that I was completely helpless. I stared into the sky. I stared into death. . . ." She paused and could not continue. She simply could not say the words.

"As they tore her apart," Siv said.

Svenka looked at her. "You know then how it is."

"Oh, yes, all too well. I saw my mate torn apart at the battle of H'rathmagyrr." She paused a moment. "And then did they take her head and fly off with it on an ice sword?"

"Yes." Svenka's voice was low and hoarse.

When the hagsfiends had left and the yellow glare had melted away, the moon once more turned silver, and Svenka awakened from her stupor. The lemmings, too, had moved on, and the great bear searched the scene of this dastardly murder for the remains of Myrrthe. What she found, which was little, was a foot with three of the four talons torn off, a wing. She buried them. But she saved one snow-white feather to bring back to Siv. She added in a growlish whisper, "And you know, Siv, the lemmings — they just kept coming and coming and coming, mindlessly racing across the land."

We were quiet for a long time after Siv had finished telling me this sad story. "You know," she finally said, "we could not have a proper Final ceremony."

"But you had one?" I asked, somewhat surprised.

"Yes. I could not bear the thought of doing nothing."

"What did you do?"

"It might seem odd, but you must understand that I still could not fly. So I climbed on top of Svenka's head and asked her to stand up. She is so tall, I might as well have been flying. The sheer immensity of this bear will never cease to amaze me. I perched as erect as I could and, holding the feather in my talons, I recited a poem I had composed in honor of Myrrthe. Then I released the feather to the winds. It floated away on the curl of a katabat, a lively, wonderfully boisterous katabat wind."

"Would you recite the poem for me now, Siv?" I asked.

"I'll try," she said, and began.

I see her in the wind,
I see her in moon's light,
I see whiteness in the dark,
I see her day and night.
When the dawn meets the morning,
when twilight slips to night,
I think of dearest Myrrthe,
a bird so white, so bright.
She is the snow of the N'yrthghar,
her whiteness curls in breaking seas.
She is everywhere I look,
but she still is lost to me.
She is the song in my heart,
she is the wind beneath my wing.
Her mercy knew no bounds,
her faith as deep as any sea.
She is everywhere I look,
yet she still is lost to me.

CHAPTER NINETEEN
The First Battle Claws

And in the far firthkin, in the ice cave of the berg while Siv herself was steeped in grief over the loss of Myrrthe, I had my talons full with young Theo. I knew that this Great Horned was an owl of unusual intelligence and extreme stubbornness. He could be absolutely maddening at times, but I had never seen an owl learn faster. To be observed by Theo is an experience in itself. He seemed to see with his entire body. If there was such a thing as a gizzard with eyes — well, that would be Theo. I, of course, kept him away from my hollow and the schneddenfyrr. Despite all the lessons and my experiments with fire, I managed to keep a close eye on the egg — so as not to arouse Theo's suspicions.

I myself knew a lot about coals and embers and flames, but Theo seemed to understand rock in ways I never imagined. First of all, he classified rocks into all sorts of categories that went way beyond the hard and soft groups into which Fengo and I used to separate the rocks during our initial experiments. He knew which rocks to use to split other rocks, and he seemed to sense just how these rocks would break when struck.

Theo often went off to look for the special rocks that he sought, ones that were extremely hard and that contained a peculiar element he called "redmor." These were the ones he wanted, and they were most often found in what Theo referred to as "weathering regions" that were near the surface of the earth. The only problem with these rocks was that the fires had to be made much hotter than normal. Oh, what I would have given for a good bonk coal! My work would have gone a lot faster. But I worked hard to keep the fires going. One day as Theo was banging away, I imagined something very different emerging from the lumpy mass he was striking.

"Theo," I said, "that prong you've got coming out there?"

"Yes," he replied. "What about it?"

It reminded me of a talon but I wasn't going to tell Theo that. Theo loved a challenge. "Can you make three more just like it? And join the four at the top?"

"Sure," he said.

One of the first tools that Theo had made were pincers, which he called "tongs." Clever gadgets, they allowed him to manipulate what he was making in the fire and then to hold it and dip it into the snow to cool it down. With his pincers, he now dipped the four-pronged object into the snow and held the finished piece up. "Pretty good, eh?"

"Excellent, lad. You are brilliant!" Theo's eyes beamed and a shiver of joy riffled through his feathers. Sometimes I wondered what kind of life Theo had had. He was so obviously smart, but had no one ever praised him? I had no idea, because Theo never spoke of his family except for that one time when he told me of his uncle the teacher. "All right. Now I have a real challenge for you."

"What is it?" His eyes blazed as brightly as the fire.

"I want you to curve those prongs at their pointy ends and make them hollow."

It took him some time, but he did it and when he stepped back, he blinked. "It looks just like a claw, almost like my talons, but more like polar bear claws," he whispered.

"Yes, Theo. You have made the first battle claws."

"I what?" He looked stunned. But I was so excited, I hardly paid attention to his reaction. "Now make another one and we'll have a pair."

"*You'll* have a pair!" he said hotly. "You seem to forget that I am a gizzard resister."

I stepped close to him. "I am not asking you to fight, Theo. I'm just asking you to make these claws. Hagsfiends are on the rise, you know this as well as I do. The coalition with Lord Arrin and Penryck is a monstrous one."

"Lord Arrin and Penryck?" Theo asked. He seemed surprised. "You mean the Sklardrog."

"Yes, precisely, the Sklardrog, the sky dragon. He has joined forces with Lord Arrin. And I repeat: I am not asking you to fight, but just to make these battle claws."

"There's no 'just' about it. 'Just' is a stupid word to use. What difference does it make if I don't fight if I provide the weapons that help owls kill each other?"

I was so exasperated. I wanted to wring his impudent neck. I squeezed my eyes shut for a long time and tried to think of a reply. There must be something I could say that might change his mind, but I didn't know what. Then it came to me: I had to tell him about the egg and whose egg it really was. I began slowly.

"Theo," I said, "I am going to tell you something that I swore I never would." He slid his head around to peer at me. I knew I had his attention. Theo's curiosity knew no bounds. "The egg in that schneddenfyrr up there." I nodded toward the tree. "It is not just any egg. It is not an ordinary egg."

"It isn't?"

Did he really know more than he was admitting to? I wasn't sure. But I had to go ahead. "This egg is the egg of the beloved King H'rath, who was slain in the battle of H'rathmagyrr, and his mate, Queen Siv." If Theo had appeared stunned before, he was now overwhelmed. "Come along, lad, I'll let you take a peek."

"You will?" He was completely astonished. I had not let him anywhere near the hollow with the schnedden-fyrr since he had arrived. He followed me up.

"Step in, young'un."

He gasped in disbelief as soon as he entered. The entire hollow was luminous from the glow of the egg. Its luster and the intensity of its luminosity had increased every day. I had never seen anything like it.

"This, Theo, is the future of our kingdom. This is a sacred charge that I have been given by Queen Siv herself. I must protect this egg at all costs. I have told you about Lord Arrin and his alliance with Penryck."

"Oh, yes," Theo replied. His voice quaked.

I felt there was more to this story than just "oh, yes," but I was not going to pursue that now. "Well," I continued, "Lord Arrin wants the egg. The hagsfiends want it. They have chased Siv halfway around the N'yrthghar. If the hagsfiends get it they will turn it to evil. With their nachtmagen, they can transform it into exactly what they are — part crow, part owl. Lord Arrin wants the egg because, as a hostage, it would be invaluable to his efforts to become the High King and rule the entire N'yrthghar. And I think he also wants it for revenge."

"Revenge?"

"Just before the battle in which H'rath was killed, his own son was killed by one of the ice harvesters who had survived the attack in the Firth of Fangs." I paused. "Killing H'rath did not seem to satisfy that vengeance he sought."

"But that is my point. Killing never satisfies. Violence simply breeds more violence."

I ignored his remarks and, looking him straight in the eyes, said, "I intend to do everything in my power to protect this egg. The queen herself has entrusted it to me. Do you know what it means for a mother to give up her chick? I am to raise him, see to his education."

"It's a male?"

"Yes." I nodded. "Theo, I am asking you to make me a pair of battle claws so I might protect this egg from destruction, to keep this hatchling from being murdered. You can see by looking at this egg that a special chick will hatch from it and — hopefully — grow into a great king. A king who can annihilate the hagsfiends — or at least nullify their magic."

The long silence in the hollow was as intense as the luminous glow from the egg. These were the longest minutes that I had ever endured. But Theo finally broke the silence. "I shall make your battle claws. But first I shall make a good hammer. Without a good hammer, I cannot make what you want. The edges must be keen, the points sharp, sharper than anything you can imagine. I need a hammer to do this."

I breathed a sigh of relief. I knew in that moment the history of warfare had been changed. We would be unleashing terrible weapons into the world of owls. We had fought only with ice before, but now we had iron, as Theo called this new metal that he had coaxed out of the black rock. Were we creating something worse than magic with these iron weapons? But by these weapons a prince might be saved. Was it worth it? I thought so. Anything that could rid the world of the nachtmagen, the horrendous magic of the hagsfiends, was worth it. And this prince was our best, our only chance.

CHAPTER TWENTY

A Stubborn Owl Gets More Stubborn

The sources for black rock were few and far between. Theo had exhausted the ones on the island in the Bitter Sea, but he felt that in the inhospitable Nameless region to the west there might be some of the rocks he needed. A particularly important ingredient was something he called "salt stars." When combined with the black rock, this salt made the metal easier to manipulate. In the Nameless region, there were said to be evaporated lakes and one small landlocked sea. He felt this would be a perfect place to find the salt stars.

"I want you to take these battle claws with you, Theo," I said.

"Why would I need battle claws in the Nameless? It's far from the war. No hagsfiends go there. It is completely empty of owls, empty of everything, except for what I seek, and no one knows that these black rocks are worth anything."

"It's not the Nameless that I worry about. It's getting there. You might encounter someone out there over the Bitter Sea."

"No one ever flies over the Bitter Sea."

"You did." I paused. "I insist. No more arguments."

He blinked. "Just one thing."

This was the most exasperating young owl I had ever met. He never gave up. I sighed. Before I could say anything, he blurted out that one more thing.

"I might have made these battle claws, but I don't know the first thing about how to use them. I have never fought in my life."

"I'm sure you'll figure out how if you have to."

"It's going to make me fly funny. I just know it. I mean, I'm adding a lot of weight. Glaux knows how I'll rudder, do a banking turn, and I can forget a steep dive for hunting prey."

"First of all, you're not wearing these on your tail feathers. So let's skip the ruddering question. Nor are you wearing them on your wings. They are to be worn over your talons. If anything, they will help you kill prey."

"It's an issue of balance."

Issue of balance! Theo always got testy when he was being challenged. "It's an *issue* of your stubbornness and your eternally argumentative nature. What we'll do, Theo," I spoke very slowly and carefully, "is have a few training sessions so you can —"

"Can what? Kill something? Kill *you*?"

At this point I exploded. "Will you kindly shut your big fat beak and listen to your elder? I should have kicked you out of here days ago!" Now he did look truly contrite.

"Sorry," he said quickly. "Go on."

"Oh, go on? You're actually giving me permission to speak? What I was going to say before you so rudely interrupted me was that you'll practice flying with them."

"All right."

"I've saved some gut and sinew from that snowshoe hare we had the other night. We'll use that to strap them on."

"Yes. That's a good idea," Theo replied. I blinked in surprise. A compliment from this youngster — rare!

"There!" I said a few minutes later as I tied the last knot. "Ready?"

"I guess so," Theo said softly.

"Come on now. Get your gizzard into this. It'll be fun."

"Fun, he calls it," Theo muttered.

"I'll ignore that!" I replied. "Now lift off from the rock on top of the forge. The heat will give you a good updraft."

A minute later, Theo was aloft. "You're doing fine," I called out.

"I might just have to keep flying over these warm updrafts forever. These things are heavy. Glaux knows what will happen if I get into cold air. The differential pressure alone will wreak havoc with my balance."

The claws had not evidently wreaked havoc with Theo's ability to talk. He kept up a steady stream as he circled over the forge. I mean, yak yak yak! No one could talk like that lad. I thought that perhaps I shouldn't worry for his safety. He could probably just talk a hagsfiend to death, should he meet one.

I knew that to nudge him out of the thermal drafts, I was going to have to be up there — right by his side. So I took off and quickly slid in next to him. "Now come on, lad, let's get you out of the thermals."

"I don't know, Grank. These things are heavy."

"Look, we'll just sort of slide into it very slowly."

"All right," he replied in a shaky voice. "Aiyeee!" He began to stagger in flight.

"Steady there! Steady!" I gave him a little bit of a wing prop by flying under him and pumping my own wings hard, sending up some puffy little pillows of air for support. "All right, you're doing fine now." Better than fine, actually. Theo was a beautiful flier. It was one of the first things that I had noticed about him shortly after he arrived. And for more than a minute now he had been flying smoothly with the added weight of the battle claws.

"I think I'll try ruddering," he said.

Ah, I thought. *He is rising to the challenge.* He began to rudder and performed an excellent banking turn.

As we settled down after our practice session, I could see that Theo was quite pleased with himself. "I don't think you need any more practice. You're a natural."

"Natural what? Killer?"

"No, no, lad, a natural flier."

"Technically speaking, we are all natural fliers, Grank."

I churred. "I'm finished arguing with you, lad. Now, on your way and here's my coal bag. Bring back a lot of rocks." I paused. "And Glaux speed!"

"Thank you, Grank. Thank you so much for everything." He paused. "And do you know what you are?"

"No, lad, what am I?"

"You're a natural-born teacher."

This indeed brought a tear to my eye.

I watched Theo take off and followed his flight as best

I could until he dissolved into a fog bank that was looming offshore. Fog sometimes unnerved me, and this one
certainly did. Who knew what might be lurking beyond
those swirling downy plumes of mist that could instantly
wrap a world in a thick impenetrable whiteness?

CHAPTER TWENTY-ONE

Siv Learns to Fly Again

"Hardly a wobble, now try a banking turn . . . little more rudder with the tail feathers, Siv."

Talk about natural-born teachers! I was nothing compared to Svenka. Imagine, if you will, Dear Owl, a polar bear teaching an owl to fly, in particular, one with a severely damaged wing. Indeed, a wing that was almost half gone!

It was most uncanny that at practically the same moment I was coaching Theo to fly with battle claws, Svenka the polar bear was attempting to teach Siv to fly again. How I first found out, or suspected this, is in itself an interesting story. For the first time in several days, I was alone. Almost as soon as Theo departed I felt a loneliness as I had never before experienced. It was not a simple loneliness. It had weight. And this weight was almost crushing me. The egg, I knew, was still several days from hatching. I decided to build a fire, not for coaxing metal out of rock but for plucking some images from the flames. For a long time I had been unwilling to peer into the flames to search for anything at all. I had become accustomed to building fires purely for utilitarian purposes. Theo was learning so fast and his research about metal was so fascinating that I had nearly forgotten that I had abilities for interpreting the flames. And to be quite frank, I was frightened. What if the fire revealed that Siv, my beloved Siv, was really dead? What then?

But within hours after Theo had left, my loneliness had turned to such despair that I built a fire. As I gazed at the soft yellow part of the flame where I often found the first glimmerings of a form I did see something. It was large and white. I peered in closer. The heat licked my face. I never had to be this close when forging, but reading was a different story. And a story was indeed unfolding before my eyes.

It was a polar bear floating lazily on her back near a large iceberg. The bear was calling instructions to a smudge in the sky high above her. As the bird spiraled down closer toward the water, I gasped. It was an owl with a badly mangled port wing and yet it was flying. And it was not just any owl. It was Siv. Dear Owl, Siv! Horrendously maimed, but still and forever Siv!

You cannot imagine my relief. The images began to fade. As was often the case after an intense, emotional reading, I was not much more than a contented, but exhausted, pile of feathers. I flew back to the hollow and basked in the glow of the egg. "You are so lucky, little one," I whispered. "Your mother, your dear mum, the most noble of owls, lives!" Did I imagine it? The light seemed to shimmer a bit as if the chick inside the egg had given the slightest little shiver.

Had the images in the flames not begun to fade I would have seen what happened next, and this would have diminished my relief and joy considerably. I only learned of it much later. There was another dark speck in the sky flying higher than Siv.

"I caught sight of him," Siv told me later, "or maybe I should say I caught the sound of his wing beats. He was flying very noisily for an owl. But I would have recognized Lord Arrin anywhere. If Lord Arrin did not personally kill H'rath, he certainly caused it, arranged it with his cohorts of hagsfiends."

As she practiced flying, Siv had been seeking out the smee holes that occurred frequently in this part of the N'yrthghar and especially in this firthkin, which was generally ice free. The steam from the smees gave her a good lift and as she was rising up on one, she heard, then spotted him. She spiraled down rapidly. She was sure that he had already seen her. There was no use hiding. Would the hagsfiends be with him? Dare they come this close to the water?

"That's him," Siv said as she lighted down at the edge of the iceberg.

"Who?" Svenka asked.

"Lord Arrin."

"The one you told me about? The one who made the alliance with the hagsfiends?"

"The one who caused my mate to die. And I think Pleek is with him."

"Pleek? Who is Pleek?" Svenka asked.

"A terrible bird. I will not deign to call him an owl. He consorts with hagsfiends." Siv gave a shudder, but then quickly recovered.

"I'll protect you, Siv. I will," Svenka said.

"He hasn't come to kill me," Siv answered.

"What did he come for then?"

"The egg."

"But it's not here,"

"He doesn't know that." Siv turned to Svenka. "And that is our only hope."

"Why is that our hope?" Svenka was confused. The polar bear knew that the strategies of owls and the politics of their world were a lot more complicated than those of polar bears.

"You see, Svenka, he thinks I have the egg. We must keep him thinking that way until the time is right."

"Right for what?" the bear asked.

"For me to get away."

"But you're still too weak."

"I know, but this is going to take more than muscle. I'm going to have to think hard about this. But get ready. He's coming in for a landing."

The immense Snowy settled between two spikes of the iceberg. "Milady." Lord Arrin nodded. "I am pleased that you are healing."

CHAPTER TWENTY-TWO

First Blood

As I rejoiced over the survival of my dear Siv, also unbeknownst to me were the trials of Theo. You see, Dear Owl, every now and then the egg had begun to make a very small rocking motion. So I knew that the time of the hatching could not be far off. I could not leave the nest to tend fires, let alone peer into them. I had gone hunting one last time to stock up on food for both the hatchling and myself. Hatchlings don't eat meat at first. We start them on insects, a few soft worms if they can be found. There were plenty of grubs and such in the tree. It was also important to keep the egg warm now. So I confined myself to the hollow. It was on the second day of this confinement period that I began to think that perhaps Theo should have returned by this time. As tempted as I might be to build a fire for flame reading, I knew that I could not let thoughts of Theo distract me. My only business now, my only reason for living, it seemed, was to see this prince into the world, to make him safe, and to teach him. Theo had said I was a natural-born teacher. This chick would be my greatest test.

I sat there for long hours on the schneddenfyrr and I wondered how far Theo had to fly for his blasted rocks. And then the next moment I would curse myself for cursing the rocks. Had I not asked him to make battle claws he never would have gone to the Nameless with its evaporated lakes and landlocked seas. Occasionally, I would drift off and dream of Theo and of battle claws. One morning at dawn, I dreamed of flames and I swear that I saw those first battle claws, which Theo was wearing, stained with blood. Was it Theo's blood? I woke up with a start. I was frightened. The wind had died down, and it was an exceptionally warm night. If I plucked more down from my own breast and tucked it in with some of the rabbit-ear moss that was abundant all over the tree, it would certainly keep the egg warm enough for a short time. I would just fly down and make a quick little fire. I simply had to. I was having very troubling thoughts about Theo. As annoying as that young'un could be, I had grown to love him as I would a son.

I gathered some peels of birch bark, which the coals always grab on to quickly, and put in some dry, well-seasoned moss. This did not need to be one of those nearly bonking fires that Theo created for his smithing. Just a small one, small but with articulate, well-shaped flames. I bent close as the first flames popped up, gasped, and drew back sharply. I blinked again and came closer. This could not be true!

Theo and a ferocious Snowy Owl were circling each other warily. The Snowy was armed with an ice saber in one talon, a short ice dagger in the other, and his beak bristled with ice splinters. The two owls were circling over a headland that jutted into the Bitter Sea. And that Snowy was not just any Snowy. It was the warlord Elgobad, cousin of Lord Arrin, and now part of that deadly pact with the hagsfiends. I knew Lord Elgobad well. In our youth, we had spent summers with our families on the same firth. He was a skillful and accomplished fighter. He was powerful — and he was a cheat. He followed no knightly rules in combat.

For there was a code of sorts. A code for noblemen and their squires and knights that defined honor on and off the battlefield. And in the flames, I saw Elgobad, true to his nature, breaking those rules. First of all, he was off the battlefield, as was Theo. He knew nothing about the battle claws, however. So, from his point of view, Theo was unarmed and Elgobad by contrast was armed quite literally to the beak. Theo himself had been staying far out of the range of engagement. He had also dipped his wings in a manner to indicate that he was not going to engage or fight. Yet Elgobad kept pressing in closer. The images in this small fire were amazingly clear. Not only were there images but I could just barely make out some brief exchanges between the two.

"Who are you and where are you going?" the Snowy Owl demanded. The sun was just setting and the fierceness of its glare on this white bird, spiky with ice weaponry, gave him a blinding radiance.

"Why do you demand to know this? This is not a war zone."

"Everywhere is a war zone."

"According to the H'rathian code of honor, the Bitter Sea is a free-fly zone."

"H'rath and his code are dead. There are new rules now. New codes. What is your name?"

Theo was silent for a long time. *Glaux!* I thought. *Now is the time to speak, lad. Say something. You who are never at a loss for words.*

"What is yours?" Theo asked.

"I am asking you. Not you me, young'un."

"If I tell you a name, how will you know it is my true name? I could tell you Glauclan or I could tell you Morfyr or I could say my name is Hegnyk —"

As the flames popped up, I could see Theo still rattling

off a dizzying number of names and flying faster and faster in circles, still out of the range for engagement. According to the H'rathian code, one who was not within range could not be considered an aggressor. It was absolutely forbidden to attack in a situation like this.

"Would you stop talking and tell me your name and where you are going?" Elgobad demanded again.

"But how would you know, I ask again, that I am not lying?"

"Nobody lies to Lord Elgobad," the Snowy screeched out.

"Oh, Lord Elgobad, so that is your name. I cannot say that I am pleased to meet you."

Lord Elgobad was stunned. How had he, the scourge of the southern N'yrthghar, been tricked by this young'un into giving his name first? He started to wilf slightly, not from fear but from shame. I knew this could turn ugly in an instant. Lord Elgobad was a bully. He would have to seek vengeance on this young owl who had embarrassed him. Just at that moment, I saw something else in the flames. I felt my gizzard seize.

This was an impossible position to be in. To be able to see so much but not help Theo was wrenching my gizzard most painfully. And I could not tear myself away from my little fire to check on the egg. The sky was growing darker. This would be the longest night of the year. I again leaned closer to the flames to get a better look at what I thought I had seen. It could be anything, anyone, but something was approaching Theo and Lord Elgobad.

The good news was that it was not a hagsfiend. The bad news was that it was one of Lord Arrin's knights. He was not armed as heavily as Elgobad, but he did fly with a very deadly looking ice scimitar. Nonetheless, the balance was hardly equal: two against one. I could only hope that this fellow had more sensitivity to the rules of war than Elgobad did.

"Who is this?" asked the newly arrived owl, a Great Horned like Theo.

"Won't tell me his name or where he is going," Elgobad answered.

"I'm a gizzard resister," Theo said. "I don't fight."

"Unless attacked!" hooted the new owl and, with that, both the Snowy and the Great Horned blasted through the purpling sky toward Theo, their ice swords, sabers, and scimitars raised.

Theo dodged them, but they quickly wheeled around and came in for a second attempt. Theo went into a giddy spiraling plunge. Then skimming close to the water, he flew as fast as any owl I had ever seen. There were few icebergs of any size in that region of the Bitter Sea but there were several ice floes, which are smaller and lower. If Theo's pursuers were hagsfiends in some sort of disguise this flight course would finish them because the wind had begun to pick up and waves were cresting and breaking, spraying salt water into the air around the floes. But they showed no fear of the sea and followed Theo as he wound in and out of the maze of ice floes. I knew that he wouldn't want to fly too far out of the Bitter Sea because then he would enter a war zone. There might be more owls, and how would he know if they were friend or foe?

The Snowy and the Great Horned were gaining on Theo as I watched. I felt my gizzard being wrenched in all directions. Suddenly, I saw a glittering missile whiz through the night, which had now turned black. It was an ice sliver and it just missed Theo's head. A sliver like that could have driven straight into his brain. Theo knew this. Suddenly, I saw him do one of the most spectacular maneuvers I have ever witnessed. It was a complete somersault in the air but executed dangerously close to the water. He came out of it and raced straight toward the two owls. His battle claws gleamed in the light of a rising moon. I heard a *whup-whup* sound. There was a terrible screech. It was all so clear that it seemed as though the fire itself was spurting blood. The breast of the Great Horned was torn open to the bone and he plummeted into the sea. The other, Lord Elgobad, went yeep, recovering just in time to fly off, looking back at Theo and his terrible claws.

The images faded. *What have I done?* I wondered. *Have I saved an owl or destroyed a gizzard resister?*

CHAPTER TWENTY-THREE
Theo Returns

"It was awful."

Those were Theo's first words when he returned. I said nothing. He looked at me. "Don't you want to know what was awful?"

"I know," I replied.

He looked surprised. "You have gone back to your fires to read the flames?"

I nodded. Early in his apprenticeship I had told Theo about my firesight and that I suspected I had lost some of my ability. It was not really the truth. The truth was that I had been frightened that I would see Siv dead in the flames. But I could not tell him that.

"I don't know why those owls were so far out in the Bitter Sea," he said.

"The Great Horned was most likely a press scout," I said.

"Press scout?"

"Owls sent out to find other owls whom they can press into soldiering."

"In other words, by killing that one owl I might have saved other owls from being forced to kill? Perhaps even saved myself from being forced to kill them?"

"Yes, exactly," I said quietly.

"And you think I should feel pleased about this?"

"I would not dare to tell you, Theo, what you should feel, but I know that it is never a good feeling to kill a living thing that is not prey to eat."

He was perched on a branch outside the hollow and he raised one talon and regarded the battle claw for several moments. The Great Horned's blood was still on it. "They will know about these now," he said. "If that owl lives to return to his troops, the word will spread. And then what will happen?"

"I don't know."

"I know," he said suddenly. "You see, Grank, we have invented a better way to kill. The whole owl world will want battle claws."

"It will take a long time, Theo. The owl world does not know about smithing. They don't know about the black rocks, about iron. It is a complicated thing you have invented. A new technology. For thousands of years we have fought with ice. And now iron? It will take time. You have a kind of genius."

"A genius for what? Killing? Don't flatter me."

"With this skill, you will make other things, not just battle claws. From copper, small containers for carrying and holding, and tools of all sorts. It will not be all battle claws."

Theo blinked at me as if to say, *You fool. You old fool!* I felt my gizzard squirm.

CHAPTER TWENTY-FOUR
A Haggish Lord

My last flame vision of Siv had been of the bear teaching her to fly. The images had faded before I saw what Siv had just spotted, and it was not until much later that I would learn what exactly had transpired, Dear Owl. But ever since Siv told me of how Lord Arrin arrived to treat with her, to make this so-called peace, the scene is vivid in my mind.

"Peace, he called it," Siv said scathingly. "It was surrender, that's what he wanted. Surrender of the egg."

"I am pleased that you are healing," the wily old bird said to Siv as he swept down to land on the berg.

Siv blinked and narrowed her eyes as she studied the leading edges of Lord Arrin's wings. No wonder she had heard him. There were no plummels. The tips of his flight feathers were ragged and dark, too dark for a Snowy. *Oh, she thought, there is something haggish about this lord, yes, very haggish, and yet he dares fly close to water.* Her gizzard shuddered. *So he is not a hagsfiend yet, just haggish enough — for now.*

Every instinct in her drove her to wilf. But she resisted. *I shall not wilf in front of this dastardly creature who calls himself an owl. I shall not wilf! Never!* And overhead, camouflaged in a thick dark cloud, she knew the haggish Pleek flew. And most likely, his mate, Ygryk, who so longed for her egg, was nearby.

Svenka had disappeared but Siv knew that she lurked close by, listening. One swipe of the polar bear's huge paw and she could decapitate this owl, but who knew what else lurked above in the clouds — Arrin's troops along with Pleek and Ygryk? Perhaps even hagsfiends ready to cast their deadly yellow light. Siv knew, as did Svenka, that it would be utter foolishness to risk an attack.

She wondered how much small talk there would be before Lord Arrin got to the point of his visit. "I see you are flying short distances. Quite amazing," he said.

"Yes, but I have always been a quick healer," Siv answered.

"Is that so? And your parents are well, I suppose." Siv remained silent. He peered at her as if expecting a response. Siv, however, was growing extremely tired of this play at civility.

"Suppose what you want about my parents, Lord Arrin. What have you come here for?"

"Oh, just to see how you are doing, to inquire about your egg and its hatching."

Aha! Siv thought. It was just as she expected. She must lie. She must fool him. For her hatchling's sake, she must keep him believing that the egg was still here. If she said anything else, Lord Arrin would launch a huge hunt for the egg. Every hagsfiend in the N'yrthghar would be summoned. Not to mention all of his own troops. They wanted that egg, that hatchling. Through that still unhatched owl, they suspected, perhaps they knew, that they could control owlkind.

You see, Dear Owl, just as I had come to know that from this egg would hatch a chick with special powers, the hagsfiends, with their own peculiar instincts, had sensed that it was special, too.

Lord Arrin asked again if the egg was near hatching.

Siv looked at the Snowy. What a vain creature he was. She could tell by the way he held himself and continued to preen when speaking to her. The cock of his head, the set of his beak, all betrayed vanity and arrogance. She sighed as if speaking to a small child and not a lord. "These things happen in their own time, Lord Arrin. You certainly must know that. They hatch when they hatch."

"But no signs yet?" he asked.

"Why should this concern you?" Siv said.

"I was only thinking, milady, how difficult it will be for you to fend for that hatchling alone, without a mate."

Thanks to you, she thought.

"You know how constantly hungry they are. You shall have to leave him to go hunting all the time."

"That is really my concern. I'll find a way, rest assured."

"I thought for your own sake, and for the safety of the chick, that you might consider some kind of a union with me, milady."

Siv was stunned. "You conveniently got rid of King H'rath, did you not? Now you propose a union with the murderer of my mate? Really, Lord Arrin!"

"It's not murder when it happens in the midst of war."

"It was murder, Lord Arrin, and you know it."

"You'll need someone, milady. You can't do it all by yourself."

Siv would not dignify his words with an answer. She simply turned away and walked back through the ice channel of the berg that led to her cave.

Siv would not come out of her cave for some time and when she did, she could not find Svenka. Instead she found a large pile of herring. She looked down at the gleaming fish. *Svenka's time must have come,* she thought. Svenka had prepared Siv for her own confinement, telling her that she would have to be gone for a few days. She had told Siv that she would need to be completely by herself, but she would leave enough fish for Siv so she wouldn't go hungry. She had explained to Siv how to dry them during that sliver of daylight between the long nights. So Siv kept herself busy laying out the small fish just as Svenka had instructed, and by practicing flying short flights. Her wing was getting stronger, there were signs of new feathers budding. And although her wing was a completely different shape, she was learning new ways to compensate for these differences through minute adjustments as she flew.

But for Siv, these nights pierced briefly by the shortest of days were the saddest time in her whole life. It was wrong, she knew, to be jealous of dear Svenka, but how could she not envy the polar bear who was about to become a mother when she herself was so far away from her own young'un? *Has he hatched yet?* she wondered. How would she ever know? And all around her, she sensed that there were other creatures giving birth, new young'uns were squirming into the world one way or another. She knew that some, like fish, hardly spent any time at all with their mothers, but others spent a great deal of time. One day, she caught a glimpse of an iceberg streaked with blood and spiraled down to see what had happened, thinking that something had been killed that would offer meat. Instead she saw a mother seal who had just given birth and was licking the filmy birth membrane off her new pups. Siv flew off immediately. She knew that they must be left alone. But her heart and gizzard were wrenching. She felt none of the joy that she knew she should have felt at seeing a new creature coming into the world. This was life, not death, and yet Siv felt only despair.

When she returned to her cave in the iceberg, she began to wonder about the blood. Why, she thought, are some animals born in a flow of blood while others are not? For Siv, it seemed very unnatural that blood should accompany the birth of anything, and she was glad it was not this way when birds hatched. *But on the other hand,* she thought, *how lovely to have your young always within you before they are even born. To feel them growing inside of you.* There was something almost miraculous about that.

Siv had much time to think during the nights and days when Svenka had gone to her birthing den. She thought about many things — the blood of birth, the transit of the stars across the sky and why they moved when they did, and why the one called Never Moves never did move. She thought a great deal about me, she said. She had known me practically her entire life. And she knew that although I possessed a certain aptitude for magic, a magic that was so different from that of the hagsfiends, at the same time I was a deep believer in reason and in what I thought of as science. She knew of my intense exploration and study of fire and flames.

So, Dear Owl, although it might seem odd, it was Siv's reflections on science and rational thought that led her to even deeper reflections on magic — not my kind of magic but the nachtmagen of the hagsfiends. What Siv began to understand about nachtmagen was far greater than any scientific discovery that I would make about fire, or Theo would make about metal.

Siv began thinking back on her own experience with the hagsfiends and how they had almost completely destroyed her. That strange paralysis that had set in; that feeling that her will was slipping away, that her gizzard had become frozen and the amazement of it all. Yes, that was the overriding emotion she had felt. Not fear, not horror, not even weakness — but amazement. And hadn't Svenka herself described that same feeling of amazement when she had looked up at the sky and seen the ragged shadows of the hagsfiends printed against the moon? *How strange*, Siv thought. She replayed in her head each minute of her own experience and compared it with much of what Svenka had described of that night when Myrrthe had been murdered.

In her own experience with the hagsfiends, she tried to recall exactly how she had first become aware of that yellow glare. Had it really flashed or had it seeped into the Ice Cliff Palace? She recalled now seeing a first dim glow looming within one of the tunnels just outside of where she and Grank had been perched by the schneddenfyrr. What she had first thought of she now realized had been distraction. Distraction, she began to think, might be the opening gambit, the first ploy of the hagsfiends. It might be the fulcrum upon which all their magic rested.

Yes! She had been distracted. That is what allowed them to ambush her and Grank so nearly fatally. But they had both escaped this first ambush. How had she done it? "Distraction!" she whispered to herself. "I distracted *them,*" She had grabbed H'rath's scimitar. They had not expected this — not from an egg-sitting mother owl. But how, she wondered — it was as if she were pushing her brain to its limits — how had they disabled her when she was pinned up against the ice wall, awash in that harsh yellow glare? And even more interesting, how had she broken through the strange powerlessness that had engulfed her?

She closed her eyes as she tried to remember those terrible endless seconds. She had felt herself going yeep.

She had felt the snow egg begin to slip and worse, she felt a kind of haggishness plucking at her gizzard. How could she, the queen of the N'yrthghar, holding the scimitar of her king and beloved mate, allow hagsfiends to tug at her gizzard, attempting to transform her into one of them? Her mind had been flooded with those thoughts. She had concentrated on those images of H'rath, she now realized. She had focused intensely on H'rath raising this scimitar in battle until those visions of him were engraved not just in her mind's eye but in her very own gizzard. It was this concentration that had made her invulnerable to their distractions. The hagsfiends had ceased to amaze her. And as they ceased to amaze her, they became ordinary and she felt her gizzard unlock. Once she could not be distracted or amazed, she was no longer theirs. Yes, it took imagination and concentration to distract them. And the odd thing was that these powers were not magical at all. They were powers that any intelligent owl might possess and might use if it dared to.

Although I agreed with Siv that her powers were not magical, I did think they were not quite as ordinary as she made them out to be. I did not believe that "any intelligent owl" could do what she had done. I felt she had Ga' deep within her gizzard. I believed that Siv was indeed a great spirit. And that great spirit was soon to be put to the test once again. Siv knew that Lord Arrin would be back, just as soon as the firthkin had frozen over. The longest night of the year was fast approaching. The day that had been merely a notch in the long night was but a sliver now. A sliver for the sunlight to pour through, hardly enough to keep the firthkin free of ice, and the warm current at this time of year swept away from Siv's iceberg in a more westerly direction, as if it were chasing the last rays of the setting sun. With the firthkin frozen solid and nary a strip of free seawater to be spied, Siv knew that Lord Arrin would return — this time with a pack of hagsfiends flying through the darkness like winged sky hounds, their fangs bared, the horrible yellow light known as the fyngrot streaming from their eyes.

CHAPTER TWENTY-FIVE

Odd Stirrings

Siv had no choice but to remain where she was. She knew that she was not yet strong enough to fly any great distance. But would she be strong enough to fend off the hagsfiends when they came? It took a different kind of strength to escape the yellow snare of the hagsfiends' nachtmagen. There had been no sign of Svenka for days. Siv had not really expected any. Svenka had told her that a mother polar bear must remain in the den with her cubs for a very long time to feed the cubs the strange liquid called milk and to share her heat with her babies who were born almost furless.

But one afternoon as the seconds peeled from the scant minutes of sunlight that remained, Siv was awakened by the sounds of cracking ice. She knew almost instantly that it was Svenka and rushed out of her hollow in the berg. There she was! Magnificent as she plowed through the ice swimming in her usual unhurried way, leaving a jagged path of open water behind her.

"Svenka! What are you doing here?"

"I have only come for a very short time."

"How are the cubs? How many? Male or female?" Siv was almost hopping up and down with the questions that came bursting out of her. "Tell me — what do they look like? Do they favor you?"

"Yes, I suppose so, though I can hardly remember their father." The casualness with which Svenka discussed this father — whoever he was — always disturbed Siv. But she knew that this was the way of polar bears. They did not mate for life as owls did.

"There were three — one died."

"Dear Glaux, how sad," Siv said.

"Not really."

Siv looked at Svenka, perplexed.

"You have to understand," Svenka continued. "Usually we give birth to just two. If there are three, there is always the risk that one will be weak and not survive. It is only because the third one died that I was able to leave for this brief time."

"How is it that you could leave?"

"I tucked First and Second around Third's body. He was still warm — warm enough to keep them warm."

"Oh." Siv paused. "First, Second, Third? Is that what you call them?"

"For now."

"Why?"

"We never name them until they have survived three moons. It makes them less . . . less . . . I don't know . . ."

"Less lovable?" Siv asked.

"I guess," Svenka said softly. "But Siv, they are so cute. It's impossible not to love them. You should see Second — she has this adorable little snubby nose, and First is a curious little fellow. That's why I must get back. They can't swim or walk. But that little fellow can still get into trouble. It's amazing. I just came to check on you."

So Siv caught her up and told her in greater detail about what she thought were Lord Arrin's plans as well as her own thoughts about magic.

Resting her elbows on the edge of the berg, Svenka took all this in and then was quiet for a long time.

"What you say about the nachtmagen is very interesting. When you describe how you were distracted and then amazed, it was very much the same with me. And you are right. Once you let them distract and then amaze you, you are theirs." Siv nodded. "And you are sure they are coming?"

"The firthkin is freezing up. When it is completely frozen, there will be no danger for the hagsfiends."

"Well, we must not permit that to happen," Svenka replied abruptly.

"How can we do that?"

"Like this!" Svenka said, and gave a mighty push away from the berg, flopped onto her back, and began wheeling her arms around. Soon there were great sounds of cracking and rumbling as the immense field of ice surrounding the berg began to split apart. She swam rapidly around the berg itself until a wide swath of open water lapped its edges. For the first time in days, Siv felt the gentle rocking motion of the iceberg floating on the billowing waters of the firthkin.

"Svenka," she said as the polar bear clambered up onto the berg. "This is wonderful. But you know how quickly it will freeze again. Perhaps the night after this when there will be no sun at all."

"I'll come back as often as I can."

"You can't leave the cubs. It's not fair to them. They are getting older and will be into more mischief."

"Indeed!" Svenka sighed. "Somehow, I'll figure out a way."

Siv sighed and felt the wonder of her Glaux-blessed life. True, she had lost her dear mate and possibly her young'un, but had she not been blessed with the most wonderful friends on earth — Myrrthe and Grank, and now Svenka?

But she counted on nothing. She knew that Svenka's first duty was to her cubs. There was no way that she could keep this region of the firthkin ice free and nurse her young'uns. Siv would have to fend for herself. As the night grew darker and darker, she watched the water grow still, until a thin coating just skimmed the surface. That coat thickened and grew silvery. The wind had died. Not a breeze riffled the surface of the firthkin's water. Indeed, it was as if everything conspired to make a pathway through these far reaches of the N'yrthghar for the hagsfiends to come directly to her. So she watched and she waited.

On the second night after Svenka had left, Siv felt odd stirrings in her gizzard. She knew that tonight was the night her son would hatch. "I knew it as surely as I had ever known anything in my life," Siv said. "He would come on this ice-sheathed, star-swirled night, the longest night of the year."

CHAPTER TWENTY-SIX
The Longest Night

I myself had waited patiently through the early winter gales wondering when this chick might hatch. In the helter-skelter of my parting from Siv at the Ice Cliff Palace, I had forgotten to ask her when exactly she had laid the egg. I had a feeling it had not been long before H'rath's death. Normally, it would take the complete moon cycle for it to hatch. But where the egg began in that cycle, I had no idea. Then one wind-bitten night, the longest night, the last night of the old owl year, when the day is but a dim thread in an endless darkness, the egg seemed to grow more luminous than ever, and I saw it jiggle forcefully. It was quickening! The jiggle then turned into a rocking motion. It was a glimmering time in this long night when the seconds slow between the last minute of the old season and the first of the new. The sky was alive with countless stars, sharp and bright, and the forest with its icy mantle caught their reflection so that it appeared as if the trunks and branches of every tree were encased in stars rather than bark.

Theo poked his head into the hollow. "He's coming, he's coming," I said.

"May I come inside?" Theo asked.

I nodded and dared not speak.

The egg rocked harder and harder. I leaned over. My gizzard jumped as I saw the minuscule point of the chick's egg tooth poke through.

I learned later that at the precise moment the chick's egg tooth pecked the shell, the hagsfiends attacked Siv.

Siv had disciplined herself to accept as nothing exceptional that first tinge of yellow that would turn the ice tawny in the night. She stood at the ready, gripping the scimitar of her mate in her talons and, most important, in her mind's eye she held the clear image of the hatching of her son. She could imagine everything about it. The egg tooth poking out, the fracture that began slowly and crept across the surface of the shell. She could imagine the tiny crackling sounds. She could even imagine the schneddenfyrr I had built but she willed herself not to imagine where it might be. This, she knew, could endanger the prince.

She had forgotten the pain in her port wing. She had forgotten yellow. It was no longer even a word in her vocabulary. It was not a color in any spectrum of color. She was filled not with hatred, not with vengeance, but love. The great spirit was flooding through her hollow bones. Her gizzard was trim and burning with Ga', her wits keen and her heart bold as she flew fearlessly out of that ice hollow in the berg with her scimitar raised to face the hagsfiends.

And this time, it was the hagsfiends who were distracted and amazed. How could this crippled owl fly? How could she blast through their awesome yellow light as if it were nothing more than the pink tinge of a summer dawn? And what was even more astounding was that in her talons she held the scimitar of H'rath. She flew directly for Penryck.

"What's happening?" Lord Arrin cried out.

I'm happening, Siv thought. She raised her scimitar and slashed at Penryck. But the hag veered off sharply. She was after him, but she began to feel an odd current in the frigid night air. It was Lord Arrin. He no longer flew like a Snowy at all. The leading edges of his flight feathers had turned even more ragged, chopping the air as he flew. She took a steep spiraling turn, plunging toward the frozen firthkin. If only there were some open water. But there was none. Ahead, everything gleamed of solid ice in the moonlight. She skimmed as close as she could, hoping that the hagsfiends — there were several now chasing her — would be too fearful of encountering an open patch of sea. They were gaining on her. And now, finally, her wing began to hurt. *I shall not be distracted! I shall not be distracted. I can fly through pain. I shall fly through pain, for my kingdom, for my son, for owlkind.* She flipped her head upward and felt her gizzard clench. Printed against the moon were the ragged shadows of three enormous hagsfiends. She was surrounded!

Had I known what was happening at the same moment the chick was hatching, I am not sure what I would have done. Instead of hagsfiends, I was seeing a little miracle happening in front of my eyes. Every hatching is in some way a miracle, a miracle that is beyond any magic. But this one in particular seemed especially miraculous when one considered the short violent history of this little chick in its egg. As soon as the egg tooth pierced the shell, a crack began to creep across the surface of the egg. The egg then gave an enormous shudder. Theo and I were rapt with attention. There was a sharp cracking sound that went on for several seconds and then, suddenly, the egg split wide open. We gasped as a featherless pale blob tumbled and flopped onto the down of the nest.

Within those same seconds when the egg split, Siv was brought down to the ice of the firthkin. She stood in a pool of moonlight, still, with her scimitar raised.

"You can't be serious, milady," Lord Arrin said, lighting several paces in front of her.

"I am deadly serious. Stand back."

"My dear," he began.

"No 'my dears,'" she shot back.

"All right, milady. Save yourself, save your young'un. Join us. You can be my lady, my queen, the queen of the nachtmagen. And here is your court." He swept a ragged wing toward the half-dozen hagsfiends who were now closing in on her.

"Never."

"We can control everything through our magic. You have already proven yourself invincible in ways that have amazed us. Is that not right, Penryck?" They came closer.

"That's right, Lord Arrin," said the foul hagsfiend, larger than the rest. He stared hard at Siv. "How ever *did* you escape the yellow fyngrot?"

She ignored the question. *They are trying to distract me,*

Siv thought. She was fully prepared at this moment to die.

"Has the chick hatched?" Lord Arrin asked.

She would not answer any questions. She was silent, silent as the night, and she stood in her silence as solid as the ice that covered the firthkin. She was completely undistractible. She could not be amazed. She was fearful of nothing except losing her son or revealing anything that might suggest that the egg was not with her, but with Grank. She knew at this moment that he had hatched. That he was alive. She and her chick might be leagues apart but they were in the same world. She felt a deeper connection with him than she had ever felt for anything before.

Lucky I had plucked my own breast feathers for the schneddenfyrr. For this little chick, and it was a male, was as naked as could be. Not a tuft of fluff on him. He was a funny little creature with his big head and bulging eyes sealed shut. Though he could barely hold that very large head up, he tried to stagger to his feet but flopped down again. Then he looked up.

"Welcome, Hoole," I whispered gently, and he cocked his head as if he were really listening, even though he could not yet see me. "Welcome, little one."

And the wind stilled and the trees stopped creaking and the very stars in the sky stopped twinkling as if holding their breath. It was as if all the world knew that something fantastic, something magical, had just happened. A small owl of great consequence and great nobility had been born.

Across the Bitter Sea, in a remote icebound firthkin, a lone Spotted Owl stood with her scimitar raised, prepared to fight to the death. She was not fearful in the least, for in her gizzard she knew that her chick had hatched, and a new life had begun.

Call me Grank. I am an old owl now. What I have told is only the beginning of the story. My writing ends here, but the story goes on. It is time for others to take up the task, others who have lived through this strange period of magic and violence.

Epilogue

Soren watched from his perch as Coryn finished reading the last page of the book. The young king closed the ancient tome and looked at Soren.

"I think I know why he wanted us to read this," Coryn said quietly.

Soren felt his gizzard give a small twinge. "Why, dear boy, why?"

"I think the ember is dangerous, very dangerous, and that is why I was destined to retrieve it before . . ." He hesitated. "Before my mother, Nyra, did. If the ember had come into her possession it would have meant . . ." Coryn looked deeply into his uncle's dark eyes. He could see his own reflection in them.

"Nachtmagen," Soren whispered.

Coryn swallowed and felt his gizzard crackle. "Yes, Soren. You know, I think, with that ember . . ." He paused and looked down at his talons. "This is very hard to say."

"Go on, my boy," Soren said gently.

"I think that ember would have released . . ." He hesitated

again. "Released something in her. Transformed her into what she truly is."

"And what would that be?" Soren asked.

"You mean, you don't know?" Coryn blinked in surprise.

"No, I don't. Tell me."

There was a deadly silence. Soren felt a twinge deep in his gizzard and leaned forward. "Tell me," he said again.

"As I said when I first came to the great tree, Soren, where there are legends, there is truth. And I have learned an unexpected truth from Grank's tale."

Coryn paused and blinked.

"My mother is a hagsfiend."

Coming soon!

GUARDIANS of GA'HOOLE

BOOK TEN

The Coming of Hoole

by Kathryn Lasky

Together Soren and Coryn open the second of three ancient volumes left to them by old Ezylryb to find a tale of heroism and treachery unfolding in a time of chaos, violence, and nachtmagen — the deadly magic of hagsfiends. It is no idle history lesson, for hidden in the legends are truths about the great promise — and great danger — that lie just ahead for the Guardians of Ga'Hoole. And so they read on:

Deep in a forest far from owls that would kill the royal hatchling, Grank raises the chick named Hoole. When a hagsfiend sent by Lord Arrin attempts to kidnap young Hoole, Grank knows that the same evil forces that killed Hrath are after the young prince. To keep him safe Grank takes him to Beyond the Beyond, a desolate land of fiery volcanoes in a barren, icy landscape. There, under Grank's guidance, Hoole will hone his mind and gizzard. But even in that strange land there are spies and traitors, and word is sent to the king-killer that a royal owl is living in Beyond the Beyond. Assassins make their way to him, but good Queen Siv in hiding has learned of these plans and makes her way to the Beyond to save her son. She must not fail, for only if the young prince lives to retrieve the one Ember will there be any hope of peace in the kingdom of owls.

About the Author

KATHRYN LASKY has long had a fascination with owls. Several years ago, she began doing extensive research about these birds and their behaviors — what they eat, how they fly, how they build or find their nests. She thought that she would someday write a nonfiction book about owls, illustrated with photographs by her husband, Christopher Knight. She realized, though, that this would be difficult since owls are nocturnal creatures, shy and hard to find. So she decided to write a fantasy about a world of owls. But even though it is an imaginary world in which owls can speak, think, and dream, she wanted to include as much of their natural history as she could.

Kathryn Lasky has written many books, both fiction and nonfiction. She has collaborated with her husband on nonfiction books such as *Sugaring Time*, for which she won a Newbery Honor; *The Most Beautiful Roof in the World*; and most recently, *Interrupted Journey: Saving Endangered Sea Turtles*. Among her fiction books are *The Night Journey*, a winner of the National Jewish Book Award; *Beyond the Burning Time*, an ALA Best Book for Young Adults; *True North; A*

Journey to the New World; *Dreams in the Golden Country*; and *Porkenstein*. She has written for the My Name Is America series, *The Journal of Augustus Pelletier: The Lewis and Clark Expedition, 1804*, and several books for The Royal Diary series, including *Elizabeth I: Red Rose of the House of Tudor, England, 1544*, and *Jahanara, Princess of Princesses, India, 1627*. She has also received *The Boston Globe* Horn Book Award as well as *The Washington Post* Children's Book Guild Award for her contribution to nonfiction.

Lasky and her husband live in Cambridge, Massachusetts.